Truth [Vérité]

Book III

by

Émile Zola

Truth [Vérité]

Book III

by Émile Zola

ISBN: 978-93-68095-80-4

Published by

DOUBLE 9 BOOKS

2/13-B, Ansari Road
Daryaganj, New Delhi – 110002
info@double9books.com
www.double9books.com
Tel. 011-40042856

ABOUT THE AUTHOR

Émile Zola was a French novelist, journalist, and the most prominent figure in the literary school of naturalism. Zola is best known for his detailed and unflinching depictions of French society. His works explore themes of social injustice, human nature, and the influence of environment and heredity on personal fate.Zola's most famous work is the Les Rougon-Macquart series, a sprawling cycle of 20 novels that trace the lives of multiple generations of a family, set against the backdrop of Second Empire France. The series includes notable works like Germinal, a powerful novel about coal miners' struggles, Thérèse Raquin, a dark tale of passion and murder, and The Downfall (La Débâcle), which explores the impact of the Franco-Prussian War. His work was a critical reflection on the failings of society, and he championed the rights of the working class and the oppressed Zola's influence on literature was immense, and his works are considered foundational to the naturalist movement.

CONTENTS

CHAPTER I

Directly the Court of Cassation started on its inquiry, David and Marc, meeting one evening in the Lehmanns' dark little shop, decided that it would be best to abstain from all agitation, and remain in the background. Now that the idea of a revision of the case was accepted, the family's great joy and hope had restored its courage. If the inquiry should be loyally conducted by the Court, Simon's innocence would surely be recognised, and acquittal would become certain. So it would suffice to remain wakeful and watchful of the march of the affair, without exhibiting any doubt of the conscientiousness and equity of the highest judges in the land.

There was only one thing which prevented the joy of those poor people from becoming perfect. The news of Simon's health was still far from good; and might he not succumb over yonder before the triumph? The Court had declared that there were no grounds for bringing him back to France before its final judgment, and it seemed likely that the inquiry might last several months. In spite of all this, however, David remained full of superb confidence, relying on the wonderful strength of resistance which his brother had hitherto displayed. He knew him, and he tranquillised the others, even made them laugh, by telling stories of Simon's youth, anecdotes which showed him retiring within himself with singular force of will, thoughtful both of his dignity and of the happiness of those near to him. So the interview between Marc, David, and the Lehmanns ended, and they separated, resolved to show neither anxiety nor impatience, but to behave as if the victory were already won.

From that time, then, Marc shut himself up in his school, attending to his pupils from morn till night, giving himself to them with an abnegation, a devotion, which seemed to increase in the midst of obstacles and suffering. While he was busy with them in the classroom, while he acted as their big brother, striving to apportion the bread of knowledge among them, he forgot some of his torture, he suffered less from the ever-bleeding wound in his heart. But in the evenings, when he found himself alone in the home whence love had fled, he relapsed into frightful despair, and wondered how it would be possible for him to continue living in dark and chilly widowerhood. Some little relief came to him on the return of Louise from

Mademoiselle Mazeline's; and yet, when the lamp had been lighted for the evening meal, what long spells of silence fell between the father and the daughter, each plunged into inconsolable wretchedness by the departure of the wife, the mother, whose desertion haunted them! They tried to escape from their pursuing thoughts by talking of the petty incidents of the day. But everything brought them back to her; they ended by talking of her alone, drawing their chairs together, and taking each other's hands, as if to warm each other in their solitude. And all their evenings ended in that fashion, the daughter seated on her father's lap with one arm around his neck, and both sobbing and quivering beside the smoky lamp. The home was dead; the absent one had carried away its life, its warmth, its light.

Yet Marc did nothing to compel Geneviève to return to him. Indeed, he did not wish to be indebted in any way to such rights as it might be possible for him to enforce. The idea of a scandal, a public dispute, was odious to him; and not only had he resolved that he would not fall into the trap set by those who had induced Geneviève to forsake him, relying in this connection on some conjugal drama which would bring about his revocation, but he also set all his hope in the sole force of love. Geneviève would surely reflect and return home. In particular, it seemed impossible that she would keep her expected child for herself alone. As soon as possible after its birth she would bring it to him, since it belonged to both of them. Even if the Church had succeeded in perverting her as a loving woman, surely it would be unable to kill her motherly feelings. And as a mother she would come back, and remain with the child. The latter's birth was near at hand, so there would not be more than a month to wait.

By degrees, after hoping for this *dénouement*, by way of consoling himself, Marc began to regard it as a certainty. And, like a good fellow, who did not wish to part mother and daughter, he sent Louise to spend Thursday and Sunday afternoons with Geneviève at Madame Duparque's, although that dark, dank, pious house had already brought him so much suffering. Perhaps he unknowingly found some last, melancholy satisfaction in this indirect intercourse, as well as a means of maintaining a tie between himself and the absent one. Whenever Louise came home after spending several hours with her mother, she brought a little of Geneviève with her; and on those evenings her father kept her longer than usual on his knees, and questioned her eagerly, longing for tidings, even though they might make him suffer.

'How did you find her to-day, my dear?' he would ask. 'Does she laugh a little? Does she seem pleased? Did she play with you?'

'No, no, father.... You know very well that she has long ceased to play. But she still had a little gaiety when she was here, and now she looks sad and ill.'

'Ill!'

'Oh! not ill enough to remain in bed. On the contrary, she cannot keep from moving about, and her hands are burning hot, as if she had the fever.'

'And what did you do, my dear?'

'We went to Vespers, as we do every Sunday. Then we returned to grandmamma's for some refreshment. There was a monk there, whom I did not know, some missionary, who told us stories of savages.'

Then Marc remained silent for a moment, full of great bitterness of spirit, but unwilling to judge the mother in the daughter's presence, or to give the latter an order to disobey her by refusing to accompany her to church. At last he resumed gently: 'And did she speak to you of me, my dear?'

'No, no, father.... Nobody there speaks to me of you, and as you told me never to speak first about you, it is just as if you did not exist.'

'All the same, grandmother is not angry with you?'

'Grandmamma Duparque hardly looks at me, and I prefer that; for she has such eyes that she frightens me when she scolds.... But Grandmamma Berthereau is very kind, especially when there is nobody there to see her. She gives me sweets, and takes me in her arms and kisses me ever so much.'

'Grandmamma Berthereau!'

'Why, yes. One day even she told me that I ought to love you very much. She is the only one who has ever spoken to me of you.'

Marc again relapsed into silence, for he did not wish his daughter to be initiated too soon into the wretchedness of life. He had always suspected that the doleful, silent Madame Berthereau, once so well loved by her husband, now led a life of agony beneath the bigoted rule of her mother, that harsh Madame Duparque. And he felt that he might possibly have an ally in the younger woman, though, unfortunately, one whose spirit was so broken that she might never find the courage to speak or act.

'You must be very affectionate with Grandmamma Berthereau,' said Marc to Louise, by way of conclusion. 'Though she may not say it, I think she is grieved as we are.... And mind you kiss your mother for both of us, she will feel that I have joined in your caress.'

'Yes, father.'

Thus did the long evening pass away, bitter but quiet, in the wrecked home. Whenever, on a Sunday, the daughter returned with some bad tidings—speaking, for instance, of a sick headache or some affection of the nerves from which the mother now suffered—the father remained full of anxiety until the ensuing Thursday. That nervous affection did not surprise him, he trembled lest his poor wife should be consumed in the perverse and imbecile flames of mysticism. But if on the following Thursday his daughter told him that mamma had smiled, and inquired about the little cat she had left at home, he revived to hope, and laughed with satisfaction and relief. Then, once again, he composed himself to await the return of the dear absent one, who would surely come back with her new-born babe at her breast.

Since Geneviève's departure Mademoiselle Mazeline, by the force of things, had become a *confidente*, an intimate for Marc and Louise. She brought the child home almost every evening, after lessons, and rendered little services in that disorganised home where there was no longer any housewife. The dwellings of the schoolmaster and the schoolmistress almost touched one another; there was only a little yard to be crossed, while in the rear a gate facilitated communication between the two gardens. Thus the intercourse became closer, particularly as Marc felt great sympathy for Mademoiselle Mazeline, whom he regarded as a most courageous and excellent woman. He had learnt to esteem her at Jonville in former times on finding that she was quite free from superstition, and strove to endow her pupils with solid minds and loving hearts. And now at Maillebois he felt intense friendship for her, so well did she realise his ideal of the educating, initiating woman, the only one capable of liberating future society. Marc was now thoroughly convinced that no serious progress would ever be effected if woman did not accompany man, and even precede him, on the road to the Happy City. And how comforting it was to meet at least one of those pioneers, one who was both very intelligent and very kind-hearted, all simplicity too, accomplishing her work of salvation as if it were one of the natural functions of her being! Thus Mademoiselle Mazeline became for Marc, amid his torture, a friend prized for her serenity and gaiety, one who imparted consolation and hope.

He was profoundly touched by the schoolmistress's sympathy and obligingness. She frequently spoke of Geneviève with anxious affection, devising excuses for her, explaining her case like a sensible woman who regarded lack of sense in others with sympathetic compassion. And she particularly begged of Marc that he would not be violent, that he would not behave like an egotistical and jealous master, one of those for whom a wife is a slave, a thing handed over to them by the laws. Without doubt Mademoiselle Mazeline had much to do with the prudence which Marc evinced in striving to remain patient and relying on sense and love to convince Geneviève and bring her back to him. Finally, the schoolmistress endeavoured with so much delicacy to replace the absent mother with Louise that she became, as it were, the light of that mournful home, where father and daughter shivered at the thought of their abandonment.

During those first fine days of the year Mademoiselle Mazeline frequently found herself of an evening with Marc and Louise in their little garden behind the school. The schoolmistress had merely to open the gate of communication, whose bolts were drawn back on either side, and neighbourly intercourse followed. Indeed she somewhat neglected her own garden for the schoolmaster's, where a table and a few chairs were set out under some lilac bushes. They jestingly called this spot 'the wood,' as if they had sought shelter under some large oaks on a patch of forest land. Then the scanty lawn was likened to a great meadow, the two flower borders became royal *parterres*; and after the day's hard work it was pleasant indeed to chat there, amid the quietude of twilight.

One evening, Louise, who had been reflecting with all a big girl's gravity, suddenly inquired: 'Mademoiselle, why have you never married?'

At this the schoolmistress laughed good naturedly. 'Oh, my darling, have you never looked at me!' she answered. 'A husband is not easily found when one has such a big nose as mine, and no figure.'

The girl looked at her mistress with astonishment, for never had she thought her ugly. True enough, Mademoiselle Mazeline did not possess a fine figure, and her nose was too large, her face a broad one, with a bumpy forehead and projecting cheek bones. But her admirable eyes smiled so tenderly that her whole countenance became resplendent with charm.

'You are very pretty,' declared Louise in a tone of conviction. 'If I were a man I should like to marry you.'

Marc felt very much amused, while Mademoiselle Mazeline gave signs of restrained emotion, tinged somewhat with melancholy. 'It would seem that the men haven't the same taste as you, my dear,' said she, as she recovered her quiet gaiety. 'When I was between twenty and twenty-five I would willingly have married, but I met nobody who wished for me. And I should not think of marrying now, when I am six and thirty.'

'Why not?' Marc inquired.

'Oh! because the time has passed.... An humble elementary teacher, born of poor parents, hardly tempts the marrying men. Where can one be found willing to burden himself with a wife who earns little, who is tied to heavy duties, and compelled to live in the depths of some out of the way region? If she is not lucky enough to marry a schoolmaster, and share her poverty with his, she inevitably becomes an old maid.... I long since gave up all idea of marriage, and I am happy all the same.'

But she quickly added: 'Of course marriage is necessary; a woman ought to marry, for she does not live, she does not fulfil her natural destiny, unless she becomes wife and mother. No real health or happiness exists for any human creature apart from his or her complete florescence. And in teaching my girls I never forget that they are destined to have husbands and children some day.... Only, when one is forgotten, sacrificed as it were, one has to arrange for oneself some little corner of content. Thus, I have cut out for myself my share of work, and I don't complain so much, for, in spite of everything, I have succeeded in becoming a mother. All the children of others, all the dear little girls with whom I busy myself from morning till evening, belong to me. I am not alone, I have a very large family.'

She laughed as she thus referred to her admirable devotion in the simple way of one who seemed to feel that she was under obligations to all the pupils who consented to become the children of her mind and heart.

'Yes,' said Marc by way of conclusion, 'when life shows itself harsh to any of us the disinherited one must behave kindly to life. That is the only way to prevent misfortune.'

On most occasions when Marc and Mademoiselle Mazeline met in the little garden, over which the twilight stole, their talk was of Geneviève. This was particularly the case on those evenings when Louise, after spending the afternoon at Madame Duparque's, returned with news of her mother. One day she came back in a state of much emotion, for her mother, whom she had accompanied to the Capuchin Chapel to witness some great ceremony in honour of St. Antony of Padua, had fainted away there, and had been carried to Madame Duparque's in a disquieting condition.

'They will end by killing her!' cried Marc despairingly.

But Mademoiselle Mazeline, wishing to comfort him, evinced stubborn optimism.

'No, no, when all is said your Geneviève has only an ailing mind, she is physically healthy and strong. Some day, you'll see, my friend, her intelligence, helped by her heart, will win the victory.... And what could you expect? She is paying for her mystical education and training in one of those convents whence, as long as they remain unclosed, the evils which assail women, and the disasters of married life, will always come. You must forgive her, she is not the real culprit. She suffers from the long heredity bequeathed to her by her forerunners, possessed, terrorised, and stupefied by the Church.'

Overcome by sadness, Marc, though his daughter was present, could not restrain a low plaint, a spontaneous avowal: 'Ah, for her sake and mine it would have been better if we had never married! She could not become my helpmate, my other self!'

'But whom would you have married, then?' the schoolmistress inquired. 'Where would you have found a girl of the middle class who had not been brought up under Catholic rule, possessed with error and falsehoods? The wife you needed, my poor friend, with your free mind—an artisan of the future as you are—still remains to be created. Perhaps just a few specimens exist, but even they are tainted by atavism and faulty education.'

Then, with a laugh, she added in her gentle yet resolute way: 'But you know that I am trying to form such companions as may be needed by the men who have freed themselves from dogmas, and who thirst for truth and equity. Yes, I am trying to provide wives for the young fellows whom you, on your side, are training.... As for yourself, my friend, you were merely born too soon.'

Thus conversing, the schoolmaster and the schoolmistress, those humble pioneers of the future social system, forgot in some measure the presence of the big girl of thirteen who listened to them in silence, but with her ears wide open. Marc had discreetly refrained from giving any direct lessons to his daughter. He contented himself with setting her an example, and she loved him dearly because he showed so much goodness of heart, sincerity, and equity. The mind of that big girl was slowly awakening to reason, but she did not dare to intervene as yet in the conversation of her father and mademoiselle; though assuredly she derived profit from it, even if, like other children, when their elders forget themselves so far as to speak before them of things regarded as being above their intelligence, she appeared neither to hear nor to understand. With her glance wandering away into the falling night, her lips scarcely stirred by a faint quiver, she was always learning, classifying in her little head all the ideas that emanated from those two persons whom, with her mother, were the ones she loved best in the world. And one day, after a conversation of the kind, a remark, which escaped her as she emerged from one of her deep reveries, showed that she had perfectly understood.

'When I marry,' said she, 'I shall want a husband whose ideas are like papa's, so that we may discuss things and come to an agreement. And if we both think alike, it will all go well.'

This manner of resolving the problem greatly amused Mademoiselle Mazeline. Marc on his side was moved, for he felt that some of his own passion for truth, his clear firm mind, was appearing in his daughter. Doubtless, while a child's brain is yet dimly developing, it is difficult to foretell what will be the woman's mature intellect. Yet Marc thought he had grounds for believing that Louise would prove sensible and healthy, free from many errors. And this probability was very sweet to him, as if indeed he awaited from his daughter the help, the loving mediation, which by bringing the absent one back to the home would re-establish all the ties so tragically severed.

However, the news which Louise brought from the Place des Capucins grew worse and worse. As the time for her child's birth drew near, Geneviève became more and more gloomy, more and more capricious and bad tempered, in such wise that at times she even rejected her daughter's caresses. She had had several more fainting fits, and was giving way, it seemed, to increasing religious exaltation, after the fashion of those patients who, disappointed by the inefficacy of certain drugs, double and double the dose until at last they poison themselves. Thus, one delightful evening, while Mademoiselle Mazeline sat with the others in the flowery garden, the news which Louise communicated rendered the schoolmistress so anxious that she made a proposal to Marc.

'Shall I go to see your wife, my friend?' she asked. 'She showed some affection for me in former times, and perhaps she might listen to me if I were to talk sense to her.'

'But what would you say to her?' Marc replied.

'Why, that her place is beside you, that she still loves you though she knows it not; that her sufferings are all due to a frightful misunderstanding; and that she will only be cured when she returns to you with that dear child, the thought of whom is stifling her like remorse.'

Tears had risen to the eyes of Marc, who felt quite upset by the schoolmistress's words. But Louise quickly intervened: 'Oh, no, mademoiselle,' she said, 'don't go to see mamma; I advise you not to.'

'Why not, my darling?'

The girl blushed, and became greatly embarrassed. She knew not how to explain in what contemptuous and hateful terms the schoolmistress was spoken of at the little house on the Place des Capucins. But Mademoiselle Mazeline understood, and, like a woman accustomed to misrepresentation, she gently asked: 'Does your mamma no longer like me, then? Do you fear she might receive me badly?'

'Oh! mamma does not say much,' Louise ended by confessing; 'it is the others.'

Then Marc, overcoming his emotion, resumed, 'The child is right, my friend. Your visit might become painful, and it would probably have no effect. None the less, I thank you for your kindness; I know how warm your heart is.'

A long spell of silence ensued. The sky overhead was beautifully clear, and quietude descended from the vast vault of azure, where the sun was expiring in a roseate flush. A few carnations, a few wallflowers, in the little garden borders perfumed the mild air. And nothing more was said that evening by Marc and his friend as they lingered, steeped in melancholy, amid the delightful close of a fine day.

The inevitable had duly come to pass. A week had not elapsed after Geneviève's departure from her home before all Maillebois was talking of a scandalous intrigue carried on publicly by the schoolmaster and the schoolmistress. In the daytime, it was said, they constantly left their classrooms to join one another, and they spent their evenings together in the garden of the boys' school, where they could be plainly distinguished from certain neighbouring windows. And the abominable thing was the constant presence of little Louise, who mingled with it all. The vilest reports speedily began to circulate. Passers-by pretended that they had heard Marc and Mademoiselle Mazeline singing, and laughing over, filthy songs. Then a legend sprang up, it being plainly established that if Geneviève had quitted her home it was in a spirit of legitimate revolt and disgust, and in order to avoid association with that other woman, that godless creature who depraved the little girls confided to her care. Thus there was not merely a question of restoring Louise to her mother; in order to save the children of Maillebois from perdition, the schoolmaster and the schoolmistress must be stoned and driven away.

Some of these rumours reached Marc's ears; but he, realising by their imbecile violence whence they emanated, merely shrugged his shoulders. As the Congregations had not managed to secure a scandal in connection with Geneviève's departure, they were resuming their underhand work of slander, striving to embitter the new state of things. They had failed to bring about Marc's revocation by taking his wife from him, but perhaps they might succeed by accusing him of keeping a mistress. Moreover, this would cast a slur on the secular schools, and was dirty work well suited to clerics who do not shrink from any lies to ensure the triumph of religion. Since the revival of the Simon case, Father Crabot, no doubt, had been leading a cloistered life, and, besides, he seemed to occupy too high a position to stoop to such abominable inventions; but all the cassocks and frocks of Maillebois were astir, Brothers and Capuchins ever winging their flight, like a covey of black gowns, over the road to Valmarie. They returned, looking very busy; and then, in all the confessional boxes of the region, in quiet corners of the chapels, and in the parlours of the convents, came endless whispering with excited female devotees, who grew terribly indignant at all the horrors they heard. Thence those horrors spread in undertones and hints to families, tradespeople, and dependents. Yet if Marc felt angry, it was only at the thought that ignoble tales were surely being whispered to Geneviève herself, in order to make their separation irrevocable.

A month elapsed, and it seemed to Marc that the birth of the expected child must be imminent. After counting the days with feverish longing he felt astonished at receiving no news, when one Thursday morning Pélagie presented herself at the school and drily requested that Mademoiselle Louise might not be sent to see her mamma that afternoon. Then, as Marc, recognising her voice, hastened to the door and demanded an explanation, the servant ended by informing him that Madame's accouchement had taken place on the Monday evening, and that she was not at all in a favourable state of health. That said, Pélagie took to her heels, feeling worried that she had spoken, for she had been told to say nothing. Marc, on his side, remained confounded. What! his wife's relations acted as if he did not exist. A child was born to him, and nobody informed him of it! And such rebellion, such a need of protest, arose within him that he at once put on his hat and repaired to the ladies' house.

When Pélagie opened the door she almost choked, thunderstruck, as she was, by his audacity. But with a wave of the arm he brushed her aside, and without a word walked into the little drawing-room where, according to their wont, Madame Duparque was knitting beside the window, while Madame Berthereau, seated a little in the rear, slowly continued some embroidery. The little room, which smelt as usual of dampness and mouldiness, seemed to be slumbering amid the deep silence and the dismal light coming from the square.

But the grandmother, amazed and indignant at the sight of Marc, sprang abruptly to her feet: 'What! you take such a liberty as this, sir! What do you want? Why have you come here?' she cried.

The incredible violence of this greeting, when Marc himself was swayed by such legitimate anger, restored his calmness.

'I have come to see my child,' he answered; 'why was I not warned?'

The old lady, who had remained rigidly erect, seemed to understand on her side also that passion might place her in a position of inferiority.

inquired. 'I am aware that you have no feelings of respect. As you deny God, how could one expect you to show any deference for a grandmother's white hair? Nevertheless, in order to show you how mistaken you are in accusing me of cloistering Geneviève, I will let you pass.... Go upstairs to her, kill her at your ease, you alone will be responsible for the fearful agony into which the sight of you will cast her.'

As she finished the old lady moved away from the door, and, returning to her seat near the window, resumed her knitting without the slightest sign of emotion, such as might have made another's hands tremble.

Marc on his side for a moment remained motionless, bewildered, at a loss what to do. Was it possible for him to see Geneviève, talk to her, strive to convince her and win her back at such a time as this? He realised how inopportune, how perilous even, such an effort would be. So without a word of adieu he slowly went towards the door. But a sudden thought made him turn.

'Since the child is no longer here, give me the address of the nurse,' he said.

Madame Duparque returned no answer, but continued to manipulate her knitting needles with her long, withered fingers in the same regular fashion as before.

'You won't give me the nurse's address?' Marc repeated.

There came a fresh pause, and at last the old woman ended by saying: 'It is not my business to give it you. Go and ask Geneviève for it, since your idea is to kill the poor child.'

Fury then overcame Marc. He sprang to the window and shouted in the grandmother's impassive face: 'You must give me the nurse's address this moment, at once!'

She, however, was still silently braving him with her clear eyes fixed upon his face when Madame Berthereau, now utterly distracted, intervened. At the outset of the dispute she had stubbornly kept her head bent over her embroidery, like one who was resigned to everything, who had become cowardly, and wished to avoid compromising herself for fear of great personal worries. But when Marc, while reproaching Madame Duparque with her harsh and fanatical tyranny, had alluded to all that she herself had suffered since her widowhood in that bigoted home, she had yielded to increasing emotion, to the tears which, long forced back, again rose from her heart and almost choked her. She forgot some of her silent timidity; after long years she raised her head once more, and became impassioned. And when she heard her mother refuse to give that poor, robbed, tortured man the address of his child's nurse, she at last rebelled, and cried the address aloud:

'The nurse is a Madame Delorme, at Dherbecourt, near Valmarie!'

At this, suddenly roused from her rigidity, Madame Duparque sprang to her feet with the nimbleness of a young woman, waving her arm the while as if to strike down the audacious creature whom she still treated as a child, though she was more than fifty years old.

'Who allowed you to speak, my girl? Are you going to relapse into your past weakness?' she cried. 'Are years of penitence powerless to efface the fault of a wicked marriage? Take care! Sin is still within you, I feel it is so, in spite of all your apparent resignation. Why did you speak without my orders?'

For a moment Madame Berthereau, who still quivered with love and pity, was able to resist. 'I spoke,' said she, 'because my heart bleeds and protests. We have no right to refuse Marc the nurse's address.... Yes, yes, what we have done is abominable!'

'Be quiet!' cried her mother furiously.

'I say that it was abominable to separate the wife from the husband, and then to separate the child from both.... Never would Berthereau, my poor dead husband, who loved me so much, never would he have allowed love to be slain like that, had he been alive.'

'Be quiet! Be quiet!'

Erect, looking taller than ever in the vigorous leanness of her three and seventy years, the old woman repeated that cry in such an imperious voice that her white-haired daughter, seized with terror, surrendered, and again bent her head over her embroidery. And heavy silence fell while she shook with a slight convulsive tremor, and tears coursed slowly down her withered cheeks, which so many other tears, shed secretly, had ravaged.

Marc had been thunderstruck by the sudden outburst of that poignant family drama, the existence of which he hitherto had merely suspected. He felt intense sympathy for that sad widow who, for more than ten years past, had been hebetated, crushed down by maternal despotism, exercised in the name of a jealous and revengeful God. And if the poor woman had not defended his Geneviève, if she had abandoned her and him to the dark fury of the terrible grandmother, he forgave her for her shuddering cowardice on seeing how greatly she suffered herself.

But Madame Duparque had again recovered her quiet composure. 'You see, sir,' she said, 'your presence here brings scandal and violence.

dark days in going, as often as possible, to see his little son Clément, at the nurse's, in that pretty village of Dherbecourt, which looked so fresh and bright amid the meadows of the Verpille, among the poplar and willow trees. He there spent a delightfully comforting hour, hoping perhaps that some happy chance would lead to a meeting with Geneviève beside the dear baby's cradle. But she was said to be still too weak to go to see her son, whom the nurse took to her on appointed days.

From that time Marc remained waiting. Nearly a year had elapsed since the Court of Cassation had begun its inquiry, which had been retarded by all sorts of complications, impeded by many obstacles, which were incessantly arising, thanks to the subterranean craft of the evil powers. At the Lehmanns' house, after the keen delight which had welcomed the first judgment ordering the inquiry, despair was reappearing now that things moved so slowly and the news of Simon was so bad. The Court, while deeming it useless to have him brought back to France immediately, had caused him to be informed that it was considering the revision of his case. But in what state would he return? Would he not succumb to his long sufferings before that constantly adjourned return could be effected? Even David, who was so firm and brave, now felt frightened. And the whole region suffered from that long wait full of anguish; it ravaged Maillebois like an exhausting crisis, the prolongation of which kept all social life in suspense. And it began to turn to the advantage of the anti-Simonists, who had recovered from the effects of the terrible discovery made at Father Philibin's. By degrees, availing themselves of the slowness of the proceedings and the false news prompted by the very secrecy of the inquiry, they again made a show of triumphing, and prophesied the certain and crushing overthrow of the Simonists. The lies and insults of great occasions again found place in the infamous articles of *Le Petit Beaumontais*. Then, at a ceremony in honour of St. Antony of Padua, Father Théodose, speaking from the pulpit, ventured to allude to God's approaching triumph over the accursed race of Judas. Brother Fulgence, also, was again seen rushing like a whirlwind along the streets and across the squares, seemingly very busy and exultant, as if indeed he were dragging the chariot of the Church behind him in some triumphal procession.

As for Brother Gorgias, whom the Congregations began to consider a very compromising personage, attempts were made to cloister him as much as possible, though his friends did not yet dare to conjure him away into some safe retreat, like Father Philibin. In this matter, as it happened, Brother Gorgias was not an easy customer to deal with, he delighted to show himself and astonish people by playing the part of a holy man who negotiated his salvation direct with Heaven. On two occasions he created a scandal by boxing the ears of some children who did not preserve a sufficiently sanctimonious demeanour on quitting the Brothers' school. Thus Mayor Philis, who, being a punctilious formalist, was scared by the other's extraordinary and violent piety, thought it his duty to intervene in the very interests of religion. The question came before the Municipal Council, where, by the way, Darras, still in a minority, was now evincing the more prudence as he did not despair of becoming Mayor again, with a larger majority than formerly, should the Simon case only turn out well. Meantime he avoided all occasions of speaking of it, keeping his lips sealed, feeling very anxious whenever he saw the monks and the priests again taking the side of the wall in Maillebois, as if it were for ever their conquered possession.

But bad though the news might be, Marc forced himself to remain hopeful. He was very much encouraged by the brave fidelity of his assistant, Mignot, who each day took a larger share in his life of devotion and battle. A singular moral phenomenon had manifested itself in this transformation in which one observed the slowly increasing influence of a master over a disciple, who at first had rebelled, then had been won back and gradually absorbed. In former times nobody would have suspected there was such heroic stuff in Mignot as now began to appear. In the affair he had behaved in a most equivocal manner, helping on the charges against Simon, and particularly endeavouring to avoid everything compromising. It had seemed as if his only thoughts were of his own advancement. Neither good nor bad, he had been liable at that time to turn out well or ill, according to circumstances and associates. And Marc had come, and had proved to be the man of intellect and will who was to decide the fate of that conscience, embellish it, and raise it to a perception of truth and justice. The lesson shone forth, luminous and positive; example, the teaching of a hero, sufficed to make other heroes arise from among the vague dim masses of average folk. On two occasions during the last ten years there had been a desire to appoint Mignot as head-master in a neighbouring little village, but he had declined the offer, preferring to remain by the side of Marc, whose influence over him had become so great that he spoke of never leaving him, of remaining to the end his faithful disciple, resolutely sharing his victory or defeat. In the same way, after postponing in a spirit of expectant prudence the question whether he would marry or not, he had decided to remain a bachelor, saying that it was too late for him to seek a wife, and that his pupils had now become his family. Besides, did he not take his meals at Marc's, where he was greeted as a brother, making that home his own, and enjoying all the delights of the nearest ties, those which are drawn closer and closer as, by degrees, one thinks and feels the same as one's fellow?

Thus the slow sundering of Marc and Geneviève had proved extremely painful to Mignot, and since Geneviève's departure he was in despair. He now again took his meals at a neighbouring eating house in order not to increase the embarrassment of that stricken home where no housewife was left. But he gave proof of respectful affection for his principal, and endeavoured to console him. If he did not join him and keep him company every evening after dinner, it was from a delicate feeling of discretion, an unwillingness to obtrude himself when Marc was alone with his daughter. He held back also when Mademoiselle Mazeline was there, feeling that she would prove more useful to the forsaken husband, more expert, with her sisterly hands, in assuaging the pain of his wounds. And when he saw Marc plunging into the deepest melancholy, ready to surrender to his sufferings, he as yet knew of only one way of bringing joy and hope to his face again, which was to reproach himself with his testimony at Simon's former trial, and vow that at the coming one he would publicly relieve his conscience and cry the truth aloud! Ah! yes, he would swear that Simon was innocent, he was convinced of it now that a stream of light had illumined his memory.

However, the slow progress made by the Court of Cassation continued to encourage the anti-Simonists in their desperate campaign, and the onslaught of slander directed against Marc became fiercer than ever. One morning a rumour spread through Maillebois that he and Mademoiselle Mazeline had been seen under circumstances which left no doubt whatever of their guilt. And ignoble particulars were given, the inventions, evidently, of overheated pious minds. At the same time the story remained unreal, for it was impossible to find a single witness, and different versions began to circulate, contradictory in character though tending to make the affair appear yet more horrible. It was Mignot who, feeling very anxious, ventured to warn Marc of the gravity of the scandal; and this time it was not sufficient for the schoolmaster to meet the ignominious charges of his enemies with the haughty silence of disdain. He spent a frightful day, wrestling with his feelings, his heart rent by the fresh sacrifice which his work demanded of him. When twilight came, however, he had made up his mind; and, according to habit, he repaired to the little garden where he spent such a pleasant and comforting hour every evening in the company of Mademoiselle Mazeline. And as she was already there, also looking very thoughtful and sad as she sat under the lilac bushes, he took a seat in front of her. For a moment he looked at her without speaking; then he said:

'My dear friend, something has happened which grieves me very much, and I wish to relieve my heart before Louise joins us.... We cannot continue meeting every day, as we have done. I even think we should do well if we abstained in future from all intercourse.... It is a question of real farewell; it is necessary we should part, my friend.'

She had listened without giving any sign of surprise; it was as if she had known beforehand what he wished to say. Indeed, in a sad but courageous voice she answered: 'Yes, my friend, it was for that very farewell that I came here this evening. There is no necessity for you to urge me to it, for, like you, I feel that it is a painful necessity.... Somebody has told me everything. In presence of such infamy our only weapons are abnegation and renouncement.'

A long interval of silence fell under the broad, calm sky, where the daylight was slowly dying. A penetrating odour came from the wallflowers, while a little freshness returned to the grass, warmed by the sunshine. And Marc resumed, in an undertone: 'Those unfortunate men who live outside the pale of simple nature and good sense can in no wise deal with man and woman without imputing to them the filth harboured by their own minds, which the idea of sin has perverted. For them woman is but a she-devil, whose contact corrupts everything—tenderness, affection, friendship.... I had foreseen what has happened, but I turned a deaf ear to it all, unwilling as I was to give them the satisfaction of seeing that I heeded their slanders. But if I myself can afford to shrug my shoulders, there is the question of you, my friend, and that of Louise, who, so I heard to-day, is likewise being assailed with this mud.... Thus they are again victorious, and will rejoice at having added another great grief to all the others.'

'For me it will be the hardest of all,' Mademoiselle Mazeline answered, with much emotion. 'I shall not merely lose the pleasure of our evening conversations; I shall have the sorrow of feeling that I am of no further use to you, and have left you yet more lonely and unhappy. Forgive me for that vain thought, my friend; but it made me so happy to help you in your work, and to fancy I gave you some comfort and support! And now I shall never think of you without picturing you forsaken, alone—even friendless.... Ah! there are certainly some very detestable people in the world.'

Marc made a trembling gesture, which betrayed his grief. 'It was what they wished to do,' said he; 'yes, they wished to isolate me and reduce me by turning every affection around me into a void. And I will admit to you that this is the only wound which really makes me suffer. All the rest, the attacks, the insults, the threats, spur me on, intoxicate me with a desire to become heroic. But to be struck in the person of those who belong to me, to see them soiled, poisoned, cast as victims among the cruelty and shame of the struggle—that is a frightful thing, which tortures me and makes me cowardly.... They have taken my poor wife, now they are separating you from me, and—I quite expect it—they will end by carrying off my daughter.'

Mademoiselle Mazeline, whose eyes were filling with tears, endeavoured to silence him. 'Take care, my friend,' she said; 'here is Louise coming.'

But he quickly retorted: 'I need not take care. I was waiting for her. She must be told what has been decided.' And as the smiling girl came forward and seated herself between them, he added: 'My darling, in a moment you must make a little nosegay for Mademoiselle. I want her to have a few of our flowers before I bolt the door between the two gardens.'

'Bolt the door—why, father?'

'Because Mademoiselle must not come here again. Our friend is being taken from us, as your mother was taken.'

Louise remained thoughtful and grave during the deep silence which followed. After looking at her father, she looked at Mademoiselle Mazeline. But she asked for no explanations; she seemed to understand, all sorts of precocious thoughts passed like faint shadows over the pure and lofty brow which she had inherited from her father, while loving distress softened her eyes.

'I will go and make the nosegay,' she said at last, 'and you shall give it to Mademoiselle, father.'

Then, while the girl went seeking the freshest flowers along the borders, the others spent a few sad yet sweet minutes together. They no longer spoke, but their thoughts mingled in brotherly, sisterly fashion, thoughts which dwelt only on the happiness of others, the reconciliation of the sexes, the education and liberation of woman, who in her turn would liberate man. And this was human solidarity in all its broadness, with all the binding and absolute ties which friendship can set between two creatures, man and woman, apart from love. He was her brother, she was his sister. Thus did they ponder; and the night, which was falling more and more swiftly over the balmy garden, brought them a restful freshness amid their sorrow.

'Here is the nosegay, father,' said Louise, approaching; 'I have tied it with a bit of grass.'

Then Mademoiselle Mazeline stood up, and Marc gave her the nosegay. All three next went towards the door. When they reached it, they remained standing there, still saying nothing, but simply feeling happy at delaying their parting for a moment. At last Marc set the door wide open, and Mademoiselle Mazeline, after passing into her own garden, turned round and, for the last time, looked at Marc, whose daughter had cast her arms about him while resting her head against his shoulder.

'Good-bye, my friend.'

'Good-bye, my friend.'

That was all, the door was slowly closed; and on either side the bolts were gently pushed forward. But they had become rusty, and raised a little plaintive cry, which seemed very sad. Everything was over, blind hatred had slain something that was good and consoling.

Another month elapsed. Marc now had only his daughter beside him, and he felt his abandonment and solitude increasing. Louise, of course, still attended Mademoiselle Mazeline's school, and under the inquisitive eyes of the girls the mistress tried to evince no preference for her, but to treat her exactly as she treated the others. The child no longer lingered behind after class-time, but hastened home to prepare her lessons beside her father. And if the schoolmaster and the schoolmistress happened to meet, they merely bowed to each other, refraining from any exchange of words, apart from such as might be necessitated by their duties.

This attitude was very much remarked and discussed in Maillebois. Reasonable people were pleased to see they did their best to put an end to the horrid reports which had been circulated: but the others sneered, saying that it was all very well to save appearances, but this did not prevent the lovers from meeting secretly. Thus infamous reports again began to circulate. When Marc heard of them from Mignot he sank into bitter discouragement. There came hours when, his courage failing, he asked of what use it was for him to wreck his life and renounce every happiness, if no sacrifice was to be held in account by the malicious. Never had his solitude been so bitter, so hard to bear. As soon as at nightfall he found himself alone with Louise in the cold, deserted house, despair came over him at the thought that if he should some day lose his child nobody would be left to love him and warm his heart.

The girl lighted the lamp and seated herself at her little table, saying: 'Papa, I am going to write my history exercise, before I go to bed.'

'That's right, my darling, work,' he answered.

Then, amid the deep silence of the empty house, anguish came upon him. He could no longer continue correcting his pupils' exercises, but rose and walked heavily up and down the room. In this wise he long went on tramping to and fro in the gloom beyond the circle of light which fell from the lamp-shade. And, at times, as he passed behind his daughter he leant over her, and brusquely kissed her hair, tears gathering the while in his eyes.

'Oh! what is the matter, papa?' asked Louise. 'You are distressing yourself again.'

A hot tear had fallen on her brow. Then, turning round, she took hold of her father with her caressing arms and compelled him to sit down near her. 'It is not reasonable of you, papa, to distress yourself like that when we are alone,' she said. 'You are so brave in the daytime, but one would think you felt frightened in the evening, just as I used to do when I did not like to remain without a light.... But as you have work to do, you ought to work.'

He tried to laugh. 'So it is you who are now the sensible grown-up person, my darling,' said he. 'But you are right, certainly; I will get to work again.'

Then, however, as he continued looking at her, his eyes again clouded, and he once more began to kiss her hair, wildly, distractedly.

'What is the matter? What is the matter?' she stammered, deeply stirred, and, in her turn, shedding tears. 'Why do you kiss me like that, papa?'

In quivering accents he then confessed his terror, acknowledged how menacing he found all the surrounding gloom: 'Ah, if at least you remain with me, my child, if at least they do not rob me of you as well.'

She could find no answer to that plaint, but she caressed him, and they wept together. At last, having succeeded in inducing him to turn to his pupils' exercises, she herself reverted to her history lesson. But when a few minutes had elapsed anxiety came on Marc again, he was compelled to rise from his chair, and walk, walk, without a pause. One might have thought he was pursuing his lost happiness athwart all the silence and darkness of his wrecked home.

Louise had lately completed her thirteenth year, so that the time when the first Communion is usually made had quite come; and all the devotees of Maillebois were indignant to see such a big girl remaining religionless, refusing to go to confession, and no longer even attending Mass. And naturally she was compassionately called a victim, crushed down beneath the brutal authority of her father, who by way of sacrilege, it was said, made her spit on the crucifix every morning and evening. Moreover, Mademoiselle Mazeline assuredly gave her lessons of diabolical depravity. But was it not a crime to leave that poor girl's soul in a state of perdition, in the power of two of the damned, whose notorious misconduct horrified every conscience? Thus, there was talk of energetic action, of organising home of the Place des Capucins would not undergo the shame of sheltering that child, its father would not soil the house by coming to kiss it, and as it would not be constantly before its mother's eyes the latter would be delivered from remorseful thoughts.

Marc, however, having by an effort calmed himself, exclaimed firmly: 'I wish to see Geneviève.'

With equal decision Madame Duparque replied: 'You cannot see her.'

'I wish to see Geneviève,' he repeated. 'Where is she? Upstairs in her old room? I shall know how to find her.'

He was already walking towards the door when the grandmother barred his passage. 'You cannot see her, it is impossible,' said she. 'You do not wish to kill her, do you? The sight of you would give her the most terrible shock. She nearly died during her accouchement. For two days past she has been pale as death, unable to speak. At the least feverishness she loses her senses, the child had to be taken away without letting her see it. Ah! you may be proud of your work; Heaven chastises all whom you have contaminated!'

Then Marc, no longer restraining himself, relieved his heart in low and quivering words: 'You evil woman! you have grown old in practising the dark cruelty of your Deity, and now you seek to annihilate your posterity.... You will pursue the work of withering your race as long as it retains in its flesh one drop of blood, one spark of human kindness. Ever since her widowhood you have banished your daughter here from life and its sweetness, you have deprived her of even the strength to speak and complain. And if your granddaughter is dying upstairs, as the result of having been wrenched from her husband and her child, it is also because you agreed to it, for you alone served as the instrument of the abominable authors of this crime.... Ah! yes, my poor, my adored Geneviève, how many lies, how many frightful impostures were needed to take her from me! And here she has been so stupefied, so perverted by black bigotry and senseless practices that she is no longer woman, nor wife, nor mother. Her husband is the devil, whom she may never see again lest she should fall into hell; her babe is the offspring of sin, and she would be in peril of damnation should she give it her breast.... Well, listen, such crimes will not be carried out to the very end. Life always regains the upper hand, it drives away the darkness and its delirious nightmares at each fresh dawn. You will be vanquished, I am convinced of it, and I even feel less horror than pity for you, wretched old woman that you are, without either mind or heart!'

Madame Duparque had listened, preserving her usual expression of haughty severity, and not even attempting to interrupt. 'Is that all!' she now

'I had no reason to warn you,' she replied; 'I was waiting for Geneviève to request me to do so.'

'And she did not ask you?'

'No.'

All at once Marc fancied that he understood the position. In the person of his wife the Church had not only striven to kill the loving woman, it had wished to kill the mother also. If Geneviève, on the eve of her delivery, had not returned to him in accordance with his hopes, if she had hidden herself away as if she were ashamed, the reason must be that her child had been imputed to her as a crime. In order to keep her in that house they must have filled her mind with fear and horror, as if she were guilty of some sin, for which she would never obtain absolution unless she severed every tie that had united her to Satan.

'Is the baby a boy?' Marc asked.

'Yes, a boy.'

'Where is he? I wish to see and kiss him.'

'He is no longer here.'

'No longer here!'

'No, he was baptised yesterday under the name of the blessed Saint Clément, and has gone away to be nursed.'

'But that is a crime!' Marc cried, with a pang of grief. 'It is not right to baptise a child without its father's consent, or to send it away, abduct it in that fashion! What! Geneviève, Geneviève, who nursed Louise with such motherly delight, is not to nurse her little Clément!'

Madame Duparque, still fully retaining her composure, gave a little grunt of satisfaction, pleased as she was in her rancour to see him suffer. 'A Catholic mother,' she answered, 'always has the right to have her child baptised, particularly when she has reason to suspect that its salvation may be imperilled by its father's atheism. And as for keeping the child here, there could be no thought of such a thing; it would have done neither the child itself, nor anybody, any good.'

Things were indeed such as Marc had fancied. The child had been regarded as the progeny of the devil, its birth had been awaited like that of Antichrist, and it had been necessary to baptise it, and send it away with all speed in order to avert the greatest misfortunes. Later, it might be taken back, an attempt might be made to consecrate it to the Deity and make a priest of it, in order to appease the divine anger. In this wise the pious little demonstrations to compel that unnatural father to restore the daughter to her mother, the pious woman whom he had driven away by the loathsome baseness of his life.

Accustomed as Marc was to insults, he only felt anxious when he thought of the violent scenes to which Louise must be subjected at the ladies' house. Her mother, still in an ailing state, was content to treat her coldly, with silent sadness, leaving Madame Duparque to thunder in the name of her angry Deity, and quicken the infernal flames under Satan's cauldrons. Ought not a big girl, already in her fourteenth year, to feel ashamed of living like a savage, like one of those dogs, who know nothing of religion and are driven from the churches? Was she not frightened by the thought of the eternal chastisement which would fall on her, the boiling oil, the iron forks, the red hot hooks, the prospect of being lacerated, boiled, and roasted during thousands after thousands of centuries? When Louise, on returning home in the evening, told Marc of those threats, he shuddered to think that such attempts should be made to capture her conscience by fright, and tried to read her eyes in order to ascertain if she were shaken.

She at times seemed moved, but then things which were really too abominable were told her. And in her quiet, sensible way she would remark: 'It is really droll, papa, that the good God should be so spiteful! Grandmamma said to-day that if I once missed going to Mass the devil would cut my feet into little pieces through all eternity.... It would be very unjust; besides, it seems to me hardly possible.'

After such remarks her father felt a little easier in mind. Unwilling as he was to do any violence to his daughter's growing intelligence, he entered into no direct discussion of the strange lessons which she received at the ladies' house; he contented himself with some general teaching, based on reason, and appealing to the child's sense of truth, justice, and kindness. He was delighted by the precocious wakening of good sense which he noticed in her, a craving for logic and certainty which she must have inherited from him. It was with joy that he saw a woman with a clear, strong mind and a tender heart already emerging from the weak girl, who still retained in many respects the childishness of her years. And if he felt anxious, it was from a fear lest the promise of a beautiful harvest should be destroyed. He only recovered his calmness when the girl astonished him by reasoning things as if she were already a grown woman full of sense.

'Oh! I am very polite, you know, with grandmamma,' she said one day. 'I tell her that if I do not go to confession or make my first Communion, it is because I am waiting till I am twenty years old, as you asked me to do.... That seems to me very reasonable. And, by keeping to that, I am very strong; for when one has reason on one's side one is always very strong, is it not so?'

At times, too, in spite of her affection and deference for her mother, she said with a smile, in a gentle, jesting way: 'You remember, papa, that mamma said she would explain the Catechism to me, and I answered her, "Yes, mamma, you shall hear me my lessons. You know that I try my best to understand." Well, as I never understood anything at the Catechism class, mamma wished to explain matters to me. But, unfortunately, I still understand nothing whatever of it.... It puts me into great embarrassment. I feel afraid I may grieve her, and all I can do is to pretend that I suddenly understand something. But I must look very stupid, for she always interrupts the lesson as if she were angry, and calls me foolish.... The other day, when she was talking of the mystery of the Incarnation, she repeated that it was not a question of understanding but of believing; and as I unluckily told her that I could not believe without understanding, she said that was one of your phrases, papa, and that the devil would take both of us.... Oh, I cried, I cried!'

She smiled, however, as she spoke of it, and added in a lower tone: 'Instead of making me think more as mamma does, the Catechism has rather taken me away from her ideas. There are too many things in it that worry my mind. It is wrong of mamma to try to force them into my head.'

Her father could have kissed her. Was he to have the joy of finding in his daughter an exception, one of those well-balanced little minds that ripen early, in which sense seems to grow as in some propitious soil? Other girls, at that troublous hour of maidenhood, are still so childish and so greatly disturbed by the quiver which comes upon them that they easily fall a prey to fairy tales and mystical reveries. How rare would be his luck if his own girl should escape the fate of her companions, whom the Church seized and conquered at a disturbing hour of life. Tall, strong, and very healthy, she was already a young woman, though there were days when she became quite childish once more, amusing herself with trifles, saying silly things, returning to her doll, with which she held extraordinary conversations. And on those days anxiety came back to her father; he trembled as he observed that there was still so much puerility in her nature, and wondered if the others might not yet steal her from him, and end by obscuring her mind, whose dawn was so limpid and so fresh.

'Ah, yes, papa, what my doll said just now was very silly! But what can you expect? She's not very sensible yet.'

'And do you hope to make her sensible, my darling?'

'I scarcely know. Her head is so hard. With Bible history she does fairly well; she can recite that by heart. But with grammar and arithmetic she is a real blockhead.'

Then she laughed. That sorry home might be empty and icy cold, she none the less filled it with childish gaiety, as sonorous as April's trumpet-wind. But the days went by, and with the lapse of time Louise became more serious and thoughtful. On returning from her Thursday and Sunday visits to her mother she sank into long, silent reveries. Of an evening, while she was working beside the lamp, she paused at times to give her father a long look, full of sorrowful affection. And at last came that which was bound to come.

It was a warm evening, and a storm was threatening, the heavens were heavy with a mass of inky clouds. The father and the daughter, according to their habit, sat working in the little circular patch of light which fell from the lamp-shade; and through the window, set wide open upon the dark and slumbering town, some moths flew in, they alone disturbing the profound silence with the slight quiver of their wings. Louise, who had spent the afternoon at the house on the Place des Capucins, seemed very tired. It was as if her brow was laden with some weighty thought. Leaning over her exercise paper, she ceased writing and reflected. And, at last, making up her mind to set down her pen, she spoke out amid the deep, mournful quietude of the house.

'Papa, I want to tell you something which grieves me very much. I shall certainly cause you very great, great sorrow; and that is why I did not have the courage to tell you of it before. But I have made up my mind now not to go to bed before telling you of what I want to do—for it seems to me so reasonable and necessary.'

Marc had immediately looked up, a pang, a feeling of terror coming to his heart, for by the girl's tremulous voice he guessed that the supreme disaster was at hand. 'What is it, my darling?' he asked.

'Well, papa, I have been turning the matter over in my head all day, and it seems to me that, if you think as I do, I ought to go and live with mamma at grandmother's.'

Marc, thoroughly upset, began by protesting violently: 'What, think as you do! No, no, I won't allow it! I mean to keep you here, I will prevent you from forsaking me.'

'Oh! papa,' she murmured distressfully, 'think it over, only just a little, and you will see that I am right.'

But he did not listen, he had risen and was walking wildly about the dim room. 'I have only you left me, and you think of going away! My wife has been taken from me, and now my daughter is to be taken, and I am to remain alone, stripped, forsaken, without an affection left! Ah! I felt that this *coup de grâce* was coming, I foresaw that those abominable hands, working in the darkness, would tear away the last shred of my heart.... But no! no! this is too much, never will I consent to such a separation!'

And stopping short before his daughter, he continued roughly: 'Have you also had your mind and heart spoilt that you no longer love me?... At each of your visits to your grandmother's I am put on trial—is it not so?—and infamous things are said about me in order to detach you from me. It is a question—eh?—of saving you from the damned and restoring you to the good friends of those ladies, who will turn you into a hypocrite and a lunatic.... And you listen to my enemies, and yield to their constant obsession by forsaking me.'

Louise, in despair, her eyes full of tears, raised her hands entreatingly. 'Papa, papa, calm yourself!' she cried. 'I assure you that you are mistaken, mamma has never allowed anything evil to be said about you before me. Grandmother, no doubt, does not like you, and she would often do well to keep quiet when I am there. It would be telling a falsehood to say that she does not do all she can to get me to join mamma and live with her. But I swear to you that neither she nor any of the others has anything to do with what I propose.... You know very well that I never tell you stories. It is I myself who have thought it all over, and come to the conclusion that our separation would be a good and sensible thing.'

'A good thing—that you should forsake me! Why, it would kill me!'

'No, you will understand—and you are so brave!... Sit down and listen to me.'

She gently compelled him to seat himself again in front of her. And, taking his hands in hers caressingly, she reasoned with him like a shrewd little woman.

'Everybody at grandmother's,' said she, 'is convinced that you alone turn me away from religion. You weigh on me, it is said, you impose your ideas on me, and if I could only escape from you I should go to confession to-morrow and make my first Communion.... So why should I not prove to them that they are mistaken? To-morrow I will go and live at grandmother's, and then they will see for themselves, they will have to admit how mistaken they have been, for nothing will prevent me from giving them always the same answer: "I have promised not to make my first Communion before I am twenty, in order that the full responsibility of such an action may be mine only, and I shall keep my promise, I shall wait."'

Marc made a gesture of doubt. 'My poor child,' said he, 'you don't know them, they will have broken down your resistance and have conquered you in a few weeks' time. You are still only a little girl.'

In her turn Louise rebelled. 'Ah! it is not nice of you, papa, to think there is so little seriousness in me! I am a little girl, it is true, but your little girl, and proud of it!'

She spoke those words with such childish bravery that he could not help smiling. That darling daughter, in whom he every now and again recognised himself, in whom he found thoughtfulness and logic blended with passionate earnestness, warmed his heart. He looked at her, and found her very pretty and very sensible, with a face which was both firm and proud, and bright eyes, whose frankness was admirable. And he continued listening while she, keeping his hands in her own, set forth the reasons which prompted her to join her mother in the devout little house of the Place des Capucins. Without any reference to the frightful slanders which were current, she let him understand that it would be well for them not to brave public opinion. As people said on all sides that her right place was at the ladies' house, she was willing to repair thither; and though she was only thirteen years of age, she would certainly be its most sensible inmate, folk would see if the work she did there did not prove the best.

'No matter, my child,' Marc said at last with an air of great lassitude, 'you will never convince me of the necessity of a rupture between you and me.'

She felt that he was weakening. 'But it is not a rupture papa,' she exclaimed; 'I have gone to see mamma twice a week, and I shall come to see you, more often than that, too.... Besides, don't you understand? Perhaps mamma will listen to me a little when I am beside her. I shall speak to her of you, I shall tell her how much you still love her, how you weep for her. And—who knows?—she will reflect, and perhaps I shall bring her back to you.'

Then the tears of both began to flow. They gave way to their emotion in each other's arms. The father was upset by the deep charm of that daughter in whom so much puerility still mingled with so much sense, goodness, and hopefulness. And the girl yielded to her heart, like one ripened before her time by things of which she was vaguely conscious, but which she would have been unable to explain.

'Do, then, as you please,' Marc ended by stammering amid his tears. 'But if I yield, don't think that I approve, for my whole being rebels and protests.'

That was the last evening they spent together. The warm night remained of an inky blackness. There seemed to be not a breath of air. And not a sound came through the open window from the resting town. Only the silent moths flew in, scorching themselves by contact with the lamp. The storm did not burst, and until very late the father and the daughter, speaking no further, remained, one in front of the other, seated at their table, as if busy with their work, but simply happy at being together yet a little longer, amid the far-spreading peaceful quietude.

How frightful, however, did the following evening prove for Marc! His daughter had left him, and he was absolutely alone in that empty and dismal dwelling. After the wife, the child—he had nobody to love him now, all his heart had been torn from him, bit by bit. Moreover, in order that he might not even have the consolation of friendship, he had been compelled, by base slanders, to cease all intercourse with the one woman whose lofty sisterly mind might have sustained him. The complete wrecking of his life, of the approach of which he had long been conscious, was now effected; the stealthy work of destruction, performed by hateful, invisible hands bent on undermining him and throwing him down on the ruins of his own work, was accomplished. And now, no doubt, the others believed they held him, bleeding from a hundred wounds, tortured and forsaken, strengthless in his blasted dwelling, that soiled and deserted home, where he was left in agony. And, indeed, on that first evening of solitude he was really a beaten man, and his enemies might well have thought him at their mercy had they been able to see him coming and going in the pale twilight with a staggering gait, like some wretched stricken beast seeking a shadowy nook there to lie down and die.

The times were, in truth, frightful. The worst possible news was current respecting the inquiry of the Court of Cassation, whose slowness seemed to hide a desire to bury the affair. In vain had Marc hitherto compelled himself to hope: each day his dread increased lest he should hear of Simon's death before the revision of the case should be an accomplished fact. During that mournful time he pictured everything as lost, revision rejected, his long efforts proving useless, truth and justice finally slain—an execrable social crime, a shameful catastrophe, which would engulf the whole country. The thought of it filled him with a kind of pious horror, sent a chilling shudder of dread through his veins. And, besides that public disaster, there was the disaster of his own life, which weighed upon him more and more. Now that Louise was no longer there, moving his heart with her charming ways, inspiriting him with her precocious sense and courage, he asked himself how he could have been mad enough to let her go to the ladies' house. She was but a child, she would be conquered in a few weeks by the all-powerful Church, which for ages past had been victorious over woman. She had been taken from him; she would never be restored to him, indeed he would never see her more. And it was he who had sent that still defenceless victim to error. His work, he himself, and those who belonged to him, were all annihilated; and at the thought of it he sank into heartrending despair.

Eight o'clock struck, and Marc had not yet found the strength to seat himself and dine alone in that room, which now had become quite dim, when he heard a timid knock at the door. And great was his astonishment when in came Mignot, who at first found it difficult to explain himself.

'You see, Monsieur Froment,' he began, 'as you announced to me this morning the departure of your little Louise, an idea came to me, and I've been turning it over in my mind all day.... So, this evening, before going to dine at the eating house——'

He paused, seeking his words.

'What, haven't you dined yet, Mignot!' Marc exclaimed.

'Why, no, Monsieur Froment.... You see, my idea was to come and dine with you, to keep you company a little. But I hesitated and lost time.... If it would please you, however, now that you are alone, I might board with you again. Two men can always agree. We could do the cooking, and surely get through the housework together. Are you agreeable? It would please me very much.'

A little joy had returned to Marc's heart; and, with a smile tinged with emotion, he replied: 'I am quite willing.... You are a good fellow, Mignot.... There, sit down, we will begin by dining together.'

And they dined, face to face, the master relapsing the while into his bitterness of spirit, the assistant rising every now and then very quietly to fetch a plate or a piece of bread, amid the melancholy calm of evening.

CHAPTER II

Then, during the months and months that the inquiry of the Court of Cassation lasted, Marc again had to shut himself up in his school, and devote himself, body and soul, to his task of instructing the humble, and rendering them more capable of truth and justice.

Among the hopes and the despairs which continued to enfever him, according as the news he heard proved good or bad, there was one thought that haunted him more and more. Long previously, at the very outset of the affair, he had wondered why France, all France, did not rise to exact the release of the innocent prisoner. One of his dearest illusions had been his belief in a generous France, a magnanimous and just France, which many times already had passionately espoused the cause of equity, and which would surely prove its goodness of heart yet once again by striving its utmost to repair the most execrable of judicial errors. And the painful surprise he had experienced on finding the country so stolid and indifferent after the trial at Beaumont now increased daily, became more and more torturing; for in the earlier stages of the affair he had been able to excuse it, realising that people were ignorant of the true facts and poisoned with lies. But now, when so much light had been cast on the affair, so much truth made manifest, he could find no possible explanation for such prolonged and such shameful slumber in iniquity. Had France been changed, then? Was it no longer the liberator? Since it now knew the truth, why did it not rise *en masse*, instead of remaining an obstacle, a blind, deaf multitude barring the road?

And Marc always returned in thought to his starting-point, when the necessity of his humble work as a schoolmaster had become apparent to him. If France still slept the heavy sleep of conscienceless matter, it was because France did not yet know enough. A shudder came upon him: how many generations, how many centuries would be needed for a people, nourished with truth, to become capable of equity? For nearly fifteen years he had been endeavouring to train up just men, a generation had already passed through his hands, and he asked himself what was really the progress that had been effected. Whenever he met any of his old pupils he chatted with them, and compared them both with their parents, who were less freed from the original clay, and with the boys who nowadays attended his school, and whom he hoped to free yet more than their forerunners. Therein lay his great task, the mission he had undertaken at a decisive hour of his life, and prosecuted throughout all his sufferings, doubting its efficacy in occasional moments of weariness, but on the morrow always taking it up again with renewed faith.

One bright August evening, having strolled along the road to Valmarie as far as Bongard's farm, Marc perceived Fernand, his former pupil, who was returning home with a scythe on his shoulder. Fernand had lately married Lucile, the daughter of Doloir, the mason; he now being five-and-twenty, and she nineteen years of age. They had long been friends, having played together in the old days on leaving school; and that evening the young wife, a little blonde, with a gentle, smiling demeanour, was also there, seated in the yard and mending some linen.

'Well, Fernand, are you satisfied? Is there a good crop of wheat this year?' Marc inquired.

Fernand still had a heavy face with a hard and narrow brow, and his words came slowly as in his childish days. 'Oh! Monsieur Froment,' he replied, 'one can never be satisfied; there's too much worry with this wretched land, it takes more than it gives.'

As his father, though barely fifty years of age, was already heavy of limb, tortured by rheumatic pains, Fernand, on finishing his term of military service, had resolved to help him, instead of seeking employment elsewhere. And the struggle at the farm was the same bitter one as of old, the family living from father to son on the fields whence it seemed to have sprung, and toiling and moiling blindly in its stubborn ignorance and neglect of progress.

'Ah! no, one is never satisfied,' Fernand slowly resumed; 'even you are not over-pleased with things, Monsieur Froment, in spite of all you know.'

Marc detected in those words some of the jeering contempt for knowledge which was to be expected from a hard-headed, sleepy dunce who in his school-days had found it difficult to remember a single lesson. Moreover, Fernand's remark embodied a prudent allusion to the events which were upsetting the whole region, and Marc availed himself of this circumstance to inquire into his former pupil's views.

'Oh! I am always pleased when my boys learn their lessons fairly well, and don't tell too many stories,' he said gaily. 'You know that very well; just remember.... Besides, I received to-day some good news about the affair to which I have been attending so long. Yes, the innocence of my poor friend Simon is about to be recognised for good.'

At this Fernand manifested great embarrassment, his countenance became heavier, and the light in his eyes died away. 'But that's not what some folk say,' he remarked.

'What do they say, then?'

'They say that the judges have found out more things about the old schoolmaster.'

'What things are those?'

'Oh, all sorts, it seems.'

At last Fernand consented to explain himself, and started on a ridiculous yarn. The Jews, said he, had given a big sum of money, five millions of francs, to their co-religionist Simon in order that he might get a Brother of the Christian Doctrine guillotined. Simon having failed in his plan, the five millions were lying in a hiding-place, and the Jews were now striving to get Brother Gorgias sent to the galleys—even if in doing so they should drown France in blood—in order that Simon might return and dig up the treasure, the hiding-place of which was known only to himself.

'Come, my lad,' Marc answered, quite aghast, 'surely you don't believe such absurdity!'

'Well, why not?' rejoined the young peasant, who looked only half awake.

'Why, because your good sense ought to rebel against it. You know how to read, you know how to write, and I flattered myself also that I had in some degree awakened your mind and taught you how to distinguish between truth and falsehood.... Come, come, haven't you remembered anything of what you learnt when you were with me?'

Fernand waved his hand in a tired, careless way. 'If one had to remember everything, Monsieur Froment, one would have one's head too full,' he said. 'I have only told you what I hear people saying everywhere. Folks who are far cleverer than I am give their word of honour that it's true.... Besides, I read something like it in *Le Petit Beaumontais* the day before yesterday. And since it's in print there must surely be some truth in it.'

Marc made a gesture of despair. What! he had not overcome ignorance more than that after all his years of striving! That young fellow remained the easiest prey for error and falsehood, he blindly accepted the most stupid inventions, he possessed neither the freedom of mind nor the sense of logic necessary to enable him to weigh the fables which he read in his newspaper. So great indeed was his credulity that it seemed to disturb even his wife, the blonde Lucile.

'Oh!' said she, raising her eyes from her work, 'a treasure of five millions, that is a great deal of money.'

Though Lucile had failed to secure a certificate, she had been one of Mademoiselle Rouzaire's passable pupils, and her mind now seemed to have awakened. It was said she was pious. In former days the schoolmistress had somewhat proudly cited her as an example, on account of the glib manner in which she recited the long Gospel narrative of the Passion without making a single mistake. But since her marriage, though one still found in her the sly submissiveness and the hypocritical restrictions of a woman on whom the Church had set its mark, she had ceased to follow the usual observances. And she even discussed things a little.

'Five millions in a hiding-place,' Marc repeated, 'five millions slumbering there, pending the return of my poor Simon—it's madness! But what of all the new documents that have been discovered, all the proofs against Brother Gorgias?'

Lucile was becoming bolder. With a pretty laugh she exclaimed: 'Oh! Brother Gorgias isn't worth much. He may well have a weight on his conscience, though all the same it would be as well to leave him quiet on account of religion.... But I've also read the newspapers, and they've made me reflect.'

'Ah! well,' concluded Fernand, 'one would never finish if one had to reflect after reading. It's far better to remain quiet in one's corner.'

Marc was again about to protest when a sound of footsteps made him turn his head, and he perceived old Bongard and his wife, who also had just returned from the fields, with their daughter, Angèle. Bongard, who had heard his son's last words, at once addressed himself to the schoolmaster.

'What the lad says is quite true, Monsieur Froment. It's best not to worry one's mind with reading so much stuff.... In my time we did not read the papers at all, and we were no worse off. Isn't that so, wife?'

'Sure it is!' declared La Bongard energetically.

But Angèle, who, in spite of her hard nut, had won a certificate at Mademoiselle Rouzaire's by force of stubbornness, smiled in a knowing manner. An inner light, fighting its way through dense matter, occasionally illumined the whole of her face, which with its short nose and large mouth remained at other moments so dull and heavy. In a few weeks' time Angèle was to marry Auguste Doloir, her sister-in-law Lucile's brother, a big strapping fellow, following, like his father, the calling of a mason, and the girl already indulged in ambitious dreams for him, some start in business on his own account when she should be beside him to guide his steps.

In response to her father's words she quietly remarked: 'Well, for my part I much prefer to know things. One can never succeed unless one does. Everybody deceives and robs one.... You yourself, mamma, would have given three *sous* too many to the tinker yesterday if I had not run through his bill.'

They all jogged their heads; and then Marc, in a thoughtful mood, resumed his walk. That farmyard, where he had just lingered for a few minutes, had not changed since the now far-distant day of Simon's arrest, when he had entered it seeking for favourable evidence. The Bongards had remained the same, full of crass, suspicious, silent ignorance, like poor beings scarce raised from the soil, who ever trembled lest they should be devoured by others bigger and stronger than themselves. And the only new element was that supplied by the children, whose progress, however, was of the slightest; for if they knew a little more than their parents they had been weakened by the incompleteness of their education, and had fallen into other imbecilities. Yet, after all, they had taken a step forward, and the slightest step forward on mankind's long road must tend to hope.

A few days later Marc repaired to Doloir's, in order to speak to him of an idea which he had at heart. Auguste and Charles, the mason's elder sons, had formerly belonged to his school, and their younger brother, Léon, [1] had lately achieved great success there, having won his certificate already in his twelfth year. For that very reason, however, he was about to quit the school, and his departure worried Marc, for, desirous as the latter was of securing good recruits for the elementary education staff, of which Salvan spoke to him at times so anxiously, he dreamt of making the lad a schoolmaster.

On reaching the flat over the wineshop in the Rue Plaisir, where the mason still dwelt, Marc found Madame Doloir alone for the moment with Léon, though the men would soon be home from work. She listened to the schoolmaster very attentively in her serious and somewhat narrow-minded way, like a good housewife who only thought of the family interests; and then she answered: 'Oh, Monsieur Froment, I don't think it possible. We shall have need of Léon: we mean to apprentice him at once. Where could we find the money to enable him to continue his studies? Things like that cost too much even when they cost nothing.' And turning to the boy she added: 'Isn't that so? A carpenter's trade suits you best. My own father was a carpenter.'

But Léon, whose eyes glittered, was bold enough to declare his preference. 'Oh no, mamma,' said he, 'I should be so pleased if I could continue learning.'

Marc was backing up the boy when Doloir came in, accompanied by his elder sons. Auguste worked for the same master as his father, and on their way home they had called for Charles, who was employed by a neighbouring locksmith. On learning what was afoot Doloir quickly sided with his wife, who was regarded as the clever one of the home, the maintainer of sound traditions. True, she was an honest and a worthy woman, but one who clung stubbornly to routine and who showed much narrow egotism. And her husband, though he put on airs of bravado, like an old soldier whose ideas had been broadened by regimental life, invariably bowed to her decisions.

> [1] In the author's proofs of the earlier part of *Vérité* Doloir the mason is said to have a young son named Léon; Savin, the clerk, having one called Jules (see *ante*, p. 60). Some confusion seems to have arisen subsequently in M. Zola's mind with respect to these boys, for in later passages of the French original the name of Jules is given to Doloir's child, and that of Léon to Savin's. This error would undoubtedly have been rectified but for M. Zola's sudden death. In the present translation Jules has been changed to Léon, and Léon to Jules, wherever necessary.—*Trans.*

'No, no, Monsieur Froment,' he said, 'I don't think it possible.'

'Come, let us reason a little,' Marc answered patiently; 'I will undertake to prepare Léon for the Training School. There we shall obtain a scholarship for him; so it will cost you absolutely nothing.'

'But what of his food all that time?' the mother asked.

'Well, just one more when there are several at table does not mean a great expense.... One may well risk a little for a child when he gives one such bright hopes.'

At this the two elder brothers began to laugh, like good-natured fellows who felt amused by the proud yet anxious bearing of their junior.

'I say, youngster, so you are to be the great man of the family, eh?' exclaimed Auguste. 'But don't put on too much side, for we won our certificates also. That sufficed for us; we had enough and to spare of all the things that one finds in books.... For my own part I much prefer to temper my mortar.' And, addressing the schoolmaster, Auguste continued gaily: 'Ah! didn't I worry you, Monsieur Froment! I could never keep still; there were days, I remember, when I revolutionised the whole class. Fortunately Charles was a little more reasonable.'

'No doubt,' said Charles, smiling in his turn, 'only I always ended by following you, for I didn't wish to be thought timid or stupid.'

'Stupid! no, no,' responded Auguste by way of conclusion: 'we were only wrong-headed and idle.... And nowadays we offer you every apology, Monsieur Froment. And I agree with you: I think that if Léon has a taste that way he ought to be helped on. Dash it all! one must be on the side of progress!'

Those words gave much pleasure to Marc, who thought it as well to rest content with them that day, and to postpone the task of finally prevailing over the parents. However, continuing his conversation with Auguste for a moment, he told him that he had lately seen his betrothed, Angèle Bongard, a shrewd little person who seemed determined to make her way in life. Then, seeing the young man laugh again and look very much flattered, Marc thought of pursuing his investigations and ascertaining what might be the views of his former pupil on the question which interested him so deeply.

'I also saw Fernand Bongard, your brother-in-law,' he said; 'you remember when he was at school with you——'

The brothers again became hilarious. 'Fernand? Oh! he had a hard nut and no mistake,' said Auguste.

'Yes, and do you know, in that unfortunate Simon affair, Fernand believes that a treasure of five millions of francs, given by the Jews, is hidden away somewhere in readiness for the unhappy prisoner whenever one may succeed in bringing him back from the galleys, and setting a Brother of the Christian Doctrine in his place.'

As these words fell from Marc's lips Madame Doloir became very grave, drawing her little figure together, and then remaining motionless; while her husband on his side made a gesture of annoyance, and muttered between his teeth: 'That's another matter which my wife rightly enough does not wish us to meddle with.'

But Auguste, who seemed very much amused, exclaimed: 'Yes, I know, the story of the treasure which appeared in *Le Petit Beaumontais*. I'm not surprised at Fernand swallowing that yarn.... Five millions hidden in the ground—it's nonsense!'

At this his father looked vexed, and emerged from his reserve. 'A treasure,' said he, 'why not? You are not so clever as you fancy, youngster. You don't know what the Jews are capable of. I knew a corporal in my regiment, who had been a servant to a Jewish banker. Well, every Saturday he saw that banker send casks full of gold to Germany—all the gold of France, as he used to say.... We are sold, that's quite certain.'

But Auguste, who never showed any great respect for anybody, retorted: 'Ah! no, father, you must not dish up the old stories of your regiment. I've just come back from barracks, you know; and it's all too stupid.... You'll soon see that for yourself, my poor Charles.'

Auguste, indeed, had lately finished his term of military service, and Charles in his turn would have to join the colours in October.

'And for my part,' Auguste continued, 'I can't swallow that absurd yarn of five millions buried at the foot of a tree, and waiting to be dug up on some moonlight night.... At the same time that does not prevent me from thinking that one would do well to leave that man Simon yonder, without troubling one's brains any more about his innocence.'

Marc, who had felt pleased by the intelligent things said by his former pupil, was painfully surprised by that sudden conclusion. 'How is that?' he inquired. 'If Simon is innocent, just think of the torture he has undergone! We should never be able to offer him sufficient reparation.'

'Oh! innocent—that remains to be proved. Though I often read what is printed, my mind only gets the more fogged by it.'

'That is because you only read falsehoods,' said Marc. 'Remember, it is now known that the copy-slip came from the Brothers' school. The corner which was torn off, and which was found at Father Philibin's, is the proof of it; and the ridiculous blunder which the experts made is demonstrated, for the paraph is certainly in the handwriting of Brother Gorgias.'

'Ah! I don't know all that,' Auguste answered. 'How can I read everything that is printed? As I said just now, the more people try to explain the affair to me, the less I understand of it. But, after all, as the experts and the Court formerly ascribed the copy-slip to the prisoner, the simplest thing is to believe that it was really his.'

From that opinion Auguste would not retreat in spite of all the efforts of Marc, who, after imagining for a moment that the young fellow possessed a free mind, was pained to discover that he had such narrow views, and such a faint perception of truth.

'Well, that is sufficient,' at last said Madame Doloir, in the authoritative manner of a prudent woman. 'You must excuse me, Monsieur Froment, if I ask you to talk no more of that affair here. You do as you please on your side, and I have nothing to say against it. Only, for poor folk like ourselves it is best that we should not meddle with what does not concern us.'

'But it would concern you, madame, if one of your sons should be taken and sent to the galleys in spite of his innocence. And we are fighting, remember, to prevent such monstrous injustice from ever being repeated.'

'Perhaps so, Monsieur Froment; but one of my sons won't be taken, for, as it happens, I try to get on well with everybody, even the priests. The priests are very strong, you see, and I would rather not have them after me.'

Thereupon Doloir was moved to intervene in a patriotic way: 'Oh! I don't care a curse about the priests,' he exclaimed. 'It's a question of defending the country, and the Government allows us to be humiliated by the English!'

'You also will please to keep quiet,' his wife immediately retorted. 'It is best to leave both the Government and the priests alone. Let's try to get bread to eat—that will be far better.'

Then Doloir had to bend his head in spite of the circumstance that among his mates he posed as being a Socialist, though he hardly knew the meaning of the word. As for Auguste and Charles, though they belonged to a better-taught generation, they sided with their mother, almost spoilt as they were by their ill-digested semi-education, too ignorant as yet to recognise the law of human solidarity which demands that the happiness of each should be compounded of the happiness of all. Only little Léon, with his ardent thirst for knowledge, remained impassioned, full of anxiety also as to the turn which things were taking.

Marc, who was sorely grieved, felt that further discussion would be useless. So, taking his departure, he contented himself with saying: 'Well, madame, I will see you again, and I hope to persuade you to allow Léon to continue his studies so that he may become a schoolmaster.'

'Quite so, Monsieur Froment,' the mother answered; 'but remember it must not cost us a *sou*, for in any case we shall be sadly out of pocket.'

Some bitter thoughts came over Marc as he returned home. As in the case of the Bongards he was reminded of the visit he had made to the Doloirs on the day of Simon's arrest. Those sorry folk, who were condemned to a life of excessive toil and who imagined they defended themselves by remaining in darkness and taking no interest in what went on around them, had in no way changed. They were determined that they would know nothing, for fear lest knowledge should bring them increase of wretchedness. The sons, no doubt, were rather more enlightened than the parents, but not enough to engage in any work of truth. And if they had begun to reason, and no longer believed in idiotic fables, how much ground there still remained for their children to cover before their minds should be freed completely from error! It was grievous indeed that the march of progress should be so slow; and yet it was necessary to remain content, if one desired to retain enough courage to pursue the arduous task of teaching and delivering the humble.

On another occasion, a little later, Marc happened to meet Savin the clerk, with whom he had had some unpleasant quarrels at the time when that embittered man's twin sons, Achille and Philippe, had attended the school. Savin had then thought it good policy to serve the Church, although he publicly pretended to have nothing to do with it, for he was continually dreading lest he should offend his superiors. However, two catastrophes, which fell upon him in rapid succession, steeped him in irremediable bitterness. First of all, things took a very bad turn with his pretty daughter, Hortense—that model pupil, in whose ardent fervour at her first Communion Mademoiselle Rouzaire had gloried, but who in reality was full of precocious hypocrisy. Savin, recognising the girl's beauty, had dreamt of marrying her to the son of one of his superiors, but, instead of that, he was compelled to marry her to a milkman's assistant, who led her astray. Then, to complete the clerk's mortification and despair, he discovered that his wife, the refined and tender-hearted Marguerite, had become unfaithful to him. In spite of her repugnance he had long compelled her to go to confession and Communion, holding that religion was a needful curb for feminine depravity; but, as it happened, her frequent attendance at the chapel of the Capuchins, whose superior, Father Théodose, was her confessor, led to her downfall, for that same holy man became her lover. The facts were never exactly known, for no scandal was raised by Savin, who, however great his rage, was overcome by the irony of things. It was he himself, indeed, who, by his imbecile jealousy, had turned his previously faithful wife into the path of infidelity. But if he raised no great outcry, people declared that he revenged himself terribly on the unhappy woman in the abominable hell which their home had now become.

Having cause to hate the priests and the monks, Savin had drawn a trifle nearer to Marc. On the day when they met in the street the clerk had just quitted his office, and was walking along with a sour and sleepy face, like some old circus horse half stupefied by his never-varying round of duties. On perceiving the schoolmaster he seemed to wake up: 'Ah! I am pleased to meet you, Monsieur Froment,' he said. 'It would be very kind of you to come as far as my rooms, for my son Philippe is causing me great anxiety by his idleness, and you are the only person who knows how to lecture him.'

'Willingly,' replied Marc, who was always desirous of seeing and judging things.

On reaching the dismal little lodging in the Rue Fauche they found Madame Savin—who still looked charming in spite of her four-and-forty years—engaged on some bead flowers which had to be delivered that same evening. Since his misfortune the clerk was no longer ashamed of letting people see his wife toil as if she were a mere workwoman. Perhaps, indeed, he hoped it would be thought that she was expiating her transgression. In former times he had evinced much pride in her when she went out wearing a lady's bonnet, but now she might well put on an apron and contribute to the support of the family. He himself also neglected his appearance, and had given up wearing frock coats.

No sooner did he enter the flat than he became brutal: 'You've taken possession of the whole room as usual!' he shouted. 'Where can I ask Monsieur Froment to sit down?'

Gentle, timid, and somewhat red of face, his wife hastened to gather up her reels and boxes. 'But when I work, my friend,' she said, 'I need some room. Besides, I did not expect you home so soon.'

'Yes, yes, I know, you never expect *me*!'

Those words, in which, perhaps, there was some cruel allusion to what had happened, quite upset the unfortunate woman. One thing which her husband did not forgive her was her lover's handsomeness, particularly as he knew that he himself was so puny and sickly; and nothing enraged himself more than to read his wife's excuse in her clear eyes. However, she now bent her head, and made herself as small as possible, while she resumed her work.

'Sit down, Monsieur Froment,' said Savin. 'As I was telling you just now, that big fellow yonder drives me to despair. He is now nearly two-and-twenty, he has already tried two or three trades, and all he seems to be good for is to watch his mother work and pass her the beads she may require.'

Young Philippe, indeed, was sitting in a corner of the room, silent and motionless, like one who strove to keep in the background. Madame Savin, amidst her humiliation, had given him a tender glance, to which he had responded by a slight smile as if by way of consolation. One could detect that he and his mother were linked together by some bond of suffering. Pale, and of poor health, the sly, cowardly, and mendacious schoolboy of former times had become a sorry young fellow, quite destitute, it seemed, of energy, who sought a refuge in his mother's kindness of heart; she, still so young in appearance, looking like an elder sister, one who also suffered, and who therefore sympathised with him.

'Why did you not listen to me?' Marc exclaimed in answer to the clerk; 'we would have made a schoolmaster of him.'

But Savin protested: 'Ah! no, indeed. Rather than that I prefer to have him on my hands. To cram one's brains at school till one is over twenty, then start at a paltry salary of sixty francs a month, and work for more than ten years before earning a hundred—do you call that a profession? A schoolmaster, indeed! Nobody cares to become one nowadays; even the poorest peasants would rather break stones on the highways!'

'But I thought I had persuaded you to let your son Jules enter the Training College?' Marc rejoined. 'Don't you intend to make him an elementary teacher?'

'Oh, dear, no. I've put him with an artificial-manure merchant. He's barely sixteen, and he is already earning twenty francs a month. He will thank me for it later on.'

Marc made a gesture expressive of his regret. He remembered having seen Jules as a babe in swaddling clothes in his mother's arms. Later, the lad, from his seventh to his fourteenth year, had become one of his pupils—a pupil who evinced much higher intelligence than his elder brothers, and who inspired great hopes. Like the master, Madame Savin, no doubt, was worried that her youngest boy's studies had been cut short by his father; for, again raising her beautiful eyes, she glanced at Marc furtively and sadly.

'Come,' said her husband to the latter, 'what advice can you give me? And first of all can't you make that big idler feel ashamed of his sloth? As you were his master, perhaps he will listen to you.'

At that moment, however, Achille, the other son, came in, returning from the process-server's office where he was now employed. He had made a start there as an errand boy when he was fifteen, and though nearly seven years had elapsed he did not yet earn enough to keep himself. Paler and of even poorer blood than his brother Philippe, he had remained a beardless stripling, sly, pusillanimous, and distrustful as in his school-days, ever ready to denounce a comrade in order to escape personal punishment. He seemed surprised on seeing his former master, and, after bowing to him, he said, doubtless in a spirit of malice: 'I don't know what there can be in *Le Petit Beaumontais* to-day, but people are almost fighting for copies at Mesdames Milhomme's. It must certainly be something more about that beastly affair.'

Marc already knew that the paper contained a fresh rectification, brimful of extraordinary mendacious impudence, on the part of Brother Gorgias; and he decided to avail himself of this opportunity to sound the young men. 'Oh!' said he, 'whatever *Le Petit Beaumontais* may attempt with its stories of buried millions, and its superb denials of well-established facts, everybody is beginning to admit that Simon is innocent.'

At this the twins shrugged their shoulders, and Achille in his drawling way replied: 'Oh! only imbeciles believe in those buried millions, and it's true that they are lying too much: one can see it. But what does it all matter to us?'

'Eh? what does it matter to you?' the schoolmaster exclaimed, surprised and failing to understand.

'Yes, what interest is there for us in that affair with which we have been plagued so long?'

Then Marc gradually became impassioned.

'My poor lads, I feel sorry for you,' he said; 'you admit Simon's innocence, do you not?'

'Well—yes. It is by no means clear, as yet; but when one has read things attentively it does seem that he may be innocent.'

'In that case, do not your feelings rebel at the idea that he is in prison?'

'Oh! it certainly isn't amusing for him,' Achille admitted; 'but there are so many other innocent people in prison. Besides, the officials may release him for all I care.... One has quite enough worries of one's own, so why should one spoil one's life by meddling with the troubles of others?'

Then Philippe, in a more gentle voice, expressed his opinion, saying: 'I don't bother about that affair, for it would worry me too much. I can understand that it would be one's duty to act if one were the master. But when one can do nothing whatever, the best way is to ignore it all and keep quiet.'

In vain did Marc censure the indifference, the cowardly egotism, and desertion which those words implied. The great voice, the irresistible will of the people, said he, was compounded of individual protests, the protests of the humblest and the weakest. Nobody could claim exemption from his duty, the action of one single isolated individual might suffice to modify destiny. Besides, it was not true to say that only one person's fate was at stake in the struggle, all the members of the nation were jointly and severally interested, for each defended his own liberty by protecting that of his fellow. And then what a splendid opportunity it was to accomplish at one stroke the work of a century of slow political and social progress. On one side all the forces of reaction were leagued against an unhappy, innocent man for the sole purpose of keeping the old Catholic and monarchical scaffoldings erect; and on the other, all who were bent on ensuring the triumph of the future, all who believed in reason and liberty, had gathered together from the four points of the compass, and united in the name of truth and justice. And an effort on the part of the latter ought to suffice to throw the former beneath the remnants of those old, worm-eaten scaffoldings which were cracking on all sides. The scope of the affair had expanded: it was no longer merely the case of a poor innocent man who had been wrongly convicted; for that man had become the incarnation of the martyrdom of all mankind, which must be wrested from the prison of the ages. The release of Simon indeed would mean increase of freedom for the people of France and an acceleration of its march towards more dignity and happiness.

But Marc suddenly lapsed into silence, for he saw that Achille and Philippe were looking at him in bewilderment, their weak eyes blinking in their pale and sickly faces.

'Oh! Monsieur Froment, what's all that? When you put so many things into the affair we can't follow you, that's certain. We know nothing of those things, we can do nothing.'

Savin for his part had listened, sneering and fidgeting, though unwilling to interrupt. Now, however, turning to the schoolmaster, he exploded. 'All that is humbug—excuse me for saying so, Monsieur Froment. Simon innocent—well, that's a matter on which I have my doubts. I don't conceal it; I'm of the same opinion as formerly, and I read nothing; I would rather let myself be killed than consent to swallow a line of all the trash that is published. And, mind, I don't say that because I like the priests. The dirty beasts—why, I wish a pestilence would sweep them all away! Only, when there is a religion, there is one. It's the same with the army. The army is the blood of France. I am a Republican, I am now a Freemason, I will go so far as to say that I am a Socialist, in the good sense of the word; but, before everything else, I am a Frenchman, and I won't have people setting their hands on what constitutes the grandeur of my country. Simon then is guilty; everything proves it: public sentiment, the proofs submitted to the Court, his condemnation, and the ignoble trafficking carried on by the Jews in order to save him. And if, by a miracle, he should not be guilty, the misfortune for the country would be too great; it would be absolutely necessary that he should be guilty all the same.'

Confronted by so much blindness, blended with so much folly, Marc could only bow. And he was about to withdraw when Savin's daughter Hortense made her appearance with her little girl Charlotte, now nearly seven years of age. Hortense was no longer the good-looking young person of former days; compelled to marry her seducer, the milkman's assistant, and lead with him a hard and toilsome life of poverty, she appeared faded and careworn. Savin, moreover, received her without cordiality, full of spite as he was, ashamed of that marriage which had mortified his pride. Only the grace and keen intelligence of little Charlotte assuaged, in some slight degree, his intensely bitter feelings.

'Good-morning, grandpapa; good-morning, grandmamma,' said the child. 'You know, I have been first in reading again, and Mademoiselle Mazeline has given me the medal.' [1]

She was a charming little girl, and Madame Savin, dropping her beads at once, took her on her lap, kissing her and feeling consoled and happy. But the child, turning towards Marc, with whom she was well acquainted, resumed: 'You know, I was the first, Monsieur Froment. It's fine—isn't it?—to be the first!'

[1] In French elementary schools the child who becomes first in his or her class is given a medal which is worn pinned to jacket or frock. Should the position be lost the medal has to be restored to the teacher, who then transfers it to the more successful pupil.—*Trans.*

'Yes, my dear,' said the master, 'it is very nice to be first. And I know that you are always very good. Mind, you must always listen to Mademoiselle Mazeline, because she will make a very clever and sensible little woman of you—one who will be very happy and who will give a deal of happiness to all her family around her.'

At this Savin again began to growl: Happiness to all her family, indeed! Well, that would be something new, for neither the grandmother nor the mother had given any happiness to him. And if Mademoiselle Mazeline should perform such a miracle as to turn a girl into something decent and useful, he would go to tell Mademoiselle Rouzaire of it. Then, annoyed at seeing his wife laugh, brightened as she was, rejuvenated, so to say, by the companionship of the child, he bade her get on with her work, speaking in so rough a voice that, as the unhappy woman again lowered her head over her bead flowers, her eyes filled with tears.

But Marc had now risen, and the clerk thereupon reverted to the matter he had at heart: 'So you can give me no advice about my big idler, Philippe?... Don't you think that, through Monsieur Salvan, who is the friend of Monsieur Le Barazer, you might get him some petty situation at the Préfecture?'

'Yes, certainly, I might try. I will speak to Monsieur Salvan about it, I promise you.'

Marc then withdrew, and, on reaching the street, walked slowly, his head bent, while he summed up the results of his visits to the parents of his former pupils. No doubt he had found Achille and Philippe possessed of riper and broader minds than Auguste and Charles, the sons of Doloir the mason, even as he had found the latter freed from the low credulity of

Fernand, the son of the peasant Bongard. But at the Savins' he had once again observed the blind obstinacy of the father, who had learnt nothing, forgotten nothing, but still lingered in the same old rut of error; whilst even the evolution of the sons towards more reason and logic remained a very slight one. Just a little step had been taken, no more, and with that Marc had to remain content. He felt sad indeed when he compared all his efforts during a period of nearly fifteen years with the little amelioration which had resulted from them. And he shuddered as he thought of the vast amount of labour, devotion, and faith which would be required throughout the humble world of the elementary teachers, before they would succeed in transforming the brutified, soiled, enthralled, lowly ones and suffering ones into free and conscious men. Generations indeed would be necessary for that to be effected.

The thought of poor Simon haunted Marc amid the grief he felt at having failed to raise a people of truth and justice, such as would have the strength of mind to rebel against the old iniquity and repair it. The nation still refused to be the noble, generous, and equitable nation, in which he had believed so long; and both his mind and his heart were pained, for he could not accustom himself to the idea of a France steeped in idiotic fanaticism. Then, however, a bright vision flitted before his eyes; he again saw little Charlotte, so wide-awake and so delighted at being the first of her class, and he began to hope once more. The future belonged to the children; and might not some of those charming little ones take giant steps when firm and upright minds should direct them towards the light?

However, as Marc drew near to the school, another meeting brought a pang to his heart. He encountered Madame Férou carrying a bundle—some work which she was taking home with her. Having lost her eldest children, who had succumbed more to want than to disease, she now lived with her remaining girl in a frightful hovel, where they worked themselves almost to death, without ever earning enough to satisfy their hunger. As she glided along the street with downcast eyes, as if ashamed of her poverty, Marc stopped her. She was no longer the plump and pleasant-looking blonde, with fleshy lips and large, bright, prominent eyes, whom he had known in past years, but a poor, squat, careworn woman, aged before her time. 'Well, Madame Férou,' he inquired, 'does the sewing prosper a little?'

She began to stammer, then at last regained some confidence: 'Oh! things never prosper, Monsieur Froment,' she said; 'we may tire our eyes out, but we are lucky when we manage to earn twenty-five *sous* a day between us.'

'And what about the application for relief which you sent to the Préfecture, as a schoolmaster's widow?'

'Oh, they never answered me, and when I ventured to call there in person, I really thought I should be arrested. A big dark man with a fine beard asked me what I meant by daring to recall the memory of my husband, the deserter and Anarchist, who was condemned by court-martial, and then shot like a mad dog. And he frightened me so much that I still tremble when I think of it.'

Then, as Marc, who was quivering, remained silent, the unhappy woman, growing bolder and bolder, resumed: 'Good heavens! My poor Férou a mad dog! You knew him when we were at Le Moreux. At first he only dreamt of devotion, fraternity, truth, and justice; and it was by dint of wretchedness, persecution, and iniquity that they ended by maddening him. When he left me, never to return, he said to me: "France is done for; it has been completely rotted by the priests, poisoned by a filthy press, plunged into such a morass of ignorance and credulity that one will never be able to extricate it!" ... And you see, Monsieur Froment, he was right!'

'No, no! He wasn't right, Madame Férou; one must never despair of one's country.'

But her blood was now up, and she retorted: 'I tell you that he *was* right! Haven't you any eyes to see? Are not affairs shameful at Le Moreux, where that man Chagnat, the creature of the priests, does nothing but debase and stupefy the children—to such a point, indeed, that for years past not a single one of them has been able to obtain a certificate of elementary studies? And then Monsieur Jauffre, your successor, does some fine work at Jonville in order to please Abbé Cognasse. At the rate they are all going, France will have forgotten how to read and write before ten years are over!'

She drew herself up as she spoke, and, consumed by hatred and rancour, the rancour of a poor downtrodden woman overcome by social injustice, she went on to prophesy: 'You hear me, Monsieur Froment. I tell you that France is done for! Nothing good nor just will ever come from her again; she will sink to the level of all those dead nations on whom Catholicism has preyed like vermin and rottenness!'

Then, still quivering with the excitement which had prompted that outburst, and trembling at having dared to say so much, she glided away with humble and anxious mien, returning to the den of suffering where her pale and silent daughter awaited her.

Marc remained confounded; it was as if he had heard Férou himself calling from his grave, crying aloud the bitter pessimism, the savage protest, dictated by the cruel sufferings of his life. And, making all allowance for rancorous exaggeration, there was great truth in the widow's words. Chagnat, indeed, was still brutifying Le Moreux, and Jauffre, under the stubborn and narrow-minded sway of Abbé Cognasse, was completing his deadly work at Jonville, in spite of the covert rage he experienced at finding that his services remained so long unrecognised, when, by rights, he ought to have been appointed at once to the headmastership of a school at Beaumont. And the great work of elementary education scarcely made more progress in any part of the region. Nearly all the schools of Beaumont were still in the power of timid masters and mistresses who, thinking of their advancement, wished to remain on good terms with the Church. Mademoiselle Rouzaire achieved great success by her devout zeal, while Doutrequin, that Republican of the early days, whom patriotic alarm had gradually cast into reaction, remained, though he was now on the retired list, a personage of great influence, one whose lofty character was cited to newcomers by way of example. How could young teachers believe in the innocence of Simon, and fight against the Congregational schools, when such a man, a combatant of 1870, a friend of the founder of the Republic, set himself on the side of the Congregations in the name of the country threatened by the Jews? For one Mademoiselle Mazeline, who ever firmly inculcated sense and kindliness, for one Mignot, won by example to the good cause, how many cowards and traitors there were, and how very slowly did the teaching staff progress in breadth of mind, generosity, and devotion, in spite of the reinforcements which came to it every year from the training schools! Yet Salvan persevered in his work of regeneration, full of ardent faith, convinced that the humble schoolmaster alone would save the country from being annihilated by the Clericals, when he himself should at last possess a free mind and the capacity to teach truth and justice. As Salvan ever repeated, the worth of the nation depended on the worth of the schoolmasters. And if the march of progress was so slow, it was because the work of evolution by which good masters might be produced had to be spread over several generations, even as several generations of pupils would be needed before a just nation, freed from error and falsehood, could spring into being.

Having reached that conclusion as the result of his inquiries and the despairing call which seemed to have come to him from Férou's grave, Marc only retained a feverish eagerness to continue the battle and increase his efforts. For some time past he had been busying himself with what were called 'after-school' enterprises, established in order to maintain a link between the masters and their former pupils, whom the laws took from them at thirteen years of age. Friendly societies were being founded on all sides, and some of the organisers dreamt of federating all those of the same *arrondissement*, then those of the same department, and finally all similar societies in France. Moreover, there were patronage societies, mutual relief and pension funds; but Marc, with the object he had in view, attached most importance to the classes for adults which he held of an evening at his school. Mademoiselle Mazeline, on her side also, had set an excellent example and won very great success by giving occasional evening lessons in cookery, family hygiene, and home nursing to those of her former pupils who were now big girls. And such numbers of young people applied to her that she ended by sacrificing her Sunday afternoons in order to instruct those who could not conveniently attend of an evening. It made her so happy, she said, to help her girls to become good wives and mothers, able to keep house and shed gaiety, health, and happiness around them.

Marc, in the same way, opened his school on three evenings every week, summoned back the boys who had left him, and endeavoured to complete their education with respect to all the practical questions of life. He sowed good seed in those young brains unsparingly, saying to himself that he would be well rewarded for his pains if but one grain out of every hundred should germinate and bear fruit. And he interested himself particularly in the few pupils whom he induced to enter the teaching profession, keeping them near him, and preparing them right zealously for the preliminary examinations at the Training College. On his side, indeed, he devoted his Sunday afternoons to those private lessons, and when evening came he was as delighted as if he had been indulging in the greatest amusement.

One of Marc's victories at this juncture was to prevail on Madame Doloir to allow him to continue educating little Léon, in order that the boy might enter the Training College in due course. The dearest of all Marc's former pupils, Sébastien Milhomme, was there already; and Sébastien's mother, Madame Alexandre, had on her side returned to the stationery shop, though she discreetly remained in the background, for fear lest she might scare away the clerical customers. And Salvan, like Marc, had now become very much attached to Sébastien, regarding him as one of those future missionaries of good tidings, whom he desired to disseminate through the country districts. Recently also, at the beginning of a new term, Marc had experienced the satisfaction of confiding to his old friend yet another pupil, none other than Joseph Simon, the innocent man's son, who, in spite of every painful obstacle, had resolved to become a schoolmaster like his father, hoping to conquer on the very field where the dear stricken prisoner had fought with so tragical a result. Thus Sébastien and Joseph had met again, each inspired with the same zeal, the same faith, their old bond of friendship tightened by yet closer sympathy than before. And what pleasant hours they spent whenever an afternoon's holiday enabled them to go to Maillebois, together, to shake hands with their former master!

While things were thus slowly moving, Marc, with respect to his home troubles, remained in suspense, one day despairing and the morrow reviving to hope. In vain had he relied on Geneviève returning to him, enlightened at last and saved from the poison; at present he set his only consolation in the quiet firmness of his daughter Louise. She, as she had promised to do, came to see him every Thursday and Sunday, invariably gay and full of gentle resolution. He dared not question her about her mother, respecting whom she seldom volunteered any information, for having no good news to give she doubtless regarded the subject as painful. Louise would now soon be sixteen, and with increase of age she became the better able to understand the cause of their sufferings. She would have been pleased indeed could she have become the mediator, the healer, the one to place the parents she loved so well in each other's arms once more. On the days when she detected extreme impatient anguish in her father's glance, she referred discreetly to the frightful situation which haunted them.

'Mamma is still very poorly,' she would say; 'it is necessary to be very careful, and I dare not as yet talk to her as to a friend. But I have hopes. There are times when she takes me in her arms, and presses me to her so tightly that I nearly suffocate, while her eyes fill with tears. At other times, it is true, she becomes harsh and unjust—accuses me of not loving her—complains, indeed, that nobody has ever loved her.... You see, father, one must be very kind to her, for she must suffer frightfully, thinking as she does that she will never more be able to content her heart.'

Then Marc, in his excitement, cried: 'But why does she not come back here? I still love her to distraction, and if she still loved me, we might be so happy.'

But Louise, in a sorrowful, gentle, caressing way, placed her hand over his mouth: 'No, no, papa, do not let us talk of that! I did wrong to begin—it can only make us grieve the more. We must wait.... I am now beside mamma; and some day she will surely see that only we two love her. She will listen to me and follow me.'

At other times the girl arrived at her father's with glittering eyes and a determined bearing, as if she had just emerged from some contest. Marc noticed it, and said to her: 'You have been disputing with your grandmother again!'

'Ah! you can see it? Well, it's true, she kept me for a good hour this morning trying to shame and terrify me about my first Communion. She speaks to me as if I were the vilest of creatures, describes to me all the abominable tortures of hell, and seems quite stupefied and scandalised by what she calls my inconceivable obstinacy.'

At this Marc brightened up, feeling somewhat reassured. He had so greatly feared that his daughter might prove as weak as other girls, and was happy to find that she remained so firm and strong-minded even when he was no longer present to support her. But emotion came upon him when he pictured her in the midst of persistent attacks, scoldings, and scenes, which left her no peace.

'My poor child!' said he, 'how much courage you need! Those constant quarrels must be very painful to you.'

But she, having now quite recovered her composure, answered, smiling: 'Quarrels? Oh! no, papa. I am too respectful with grandmamma to quarrel with her. It is she who is always getting angry and threatening me. I listen to her very deferentially, without ever making the slightest interruption. And when she has quite finished, after beginning two or three times afresh, I content myself with saying very gently: "But how can I help it, grandmamma? I promised papa that I would wait until I was twenty before deciding whether I would make my first Communion or not; and as I swore it, I will keep my word." You see, I never depart from that answer. I know it by heart, and repeat it without changing a word. That makes me invincible. And I sometimes begin to pity poor grandmamma, for she flies into such a temper, banging the door in my face as soon as ever I begin that phrase!'

In the depths of her heart Louise suffered from that perpetual warfare; but on observing her father's delight, she prettily cast her arms around his neck, and added, 'You see, you may be quite easy, I am really your daughter. Nobody will ever make me do anything when I have decided that I won't do it!'

The girl also had to carry on a battle with her grandmother in order to continue her studies, resolved as she was to devote herself to the teaching profession. In this respect she fortunately had the support of her mother, who regarded the future as being very uncertain by reason of the increasing avarice which Madame Duparque displayed towards her family. The old lady preferred to devote her little fortune to pious works; and since giving an asylum to Geneviève and her daughter she had insisted upon their paying for their board, in this respect wishing to annoy Marc, who consequently had to make his wife a considerable allowance out of his meagre salary. Perhaps Madame Duparque—advised in this matter as in others by her good friends, those masters of intrigue, whose unseen hands pulled every string—had hoped that Marc would respond by a refusal, and that a scandal would ensue. But he could live on very little, and he consented immediately, as if indeed he were well pleased to remain the paterfamilias, the worker, and supporter of those who belonged to him. And although straitened circumstances aggravated his solitude, the meals he shared with Mignot becoming extremely frugal, he did not suffer, for it was sufficient for him to know that Geneviève had appeared moved by his willingness to provide for her, and that she found in this pecuniary question a motive to approve of Louise's resolution to pursue her studies in order to ensure her future. Thus the girl, who had already obtained her elementary certificate, continued to take lessons from Mademoiselle Mazeline, preparing herself for the superior certificate examination, which circumstance gave rise to further disputes with Madame Duparque, who was exasperated by all the science which it had become the fashion to impart to young girls, when, in her opinion, the catechism ought to have sufficed them. And as Louise always answered every protest in her extremely deferential manner: 'Yes, grandmamma; certainly, grandmamma,' the old lady grew more exasperated than ever, and ended by picking quarrels with Geneviève, who, losing patience, occasionally answered back.

One day while Marc was listening to the news his daughter gave him, he became quite astonished. 'Does mamma quarrel with grandmother then?' he inquired.

'Oh, yes, papa. This was even the second or third time. And mamma, you know, does not beat about the bush. She loses her temper at once, answers back in a loud voice, and then goes to sulk in her room as she used to do here before she left.'

Marc listened, unwilling to give utterance to the secret delight, the hope, which was rising within him.

'And does Madame Berthereau take part in these discussions?' he resumed.

'Oh, grandmamma Berthereau never says anything. She sides with mamma and me, I think; but she does not dare to support us openly for fear of worries.... She looks very sad and very ailing.'

However, months went by, and Marc saw none of his hopes fulfilled. It must be said that he observed great discretion in questioning his daughter, for it was repugnant to him to turn her into a kind of spy for the purpose of keeping himself informed of everything that occurred in the dismal little house on the Place des Capucins. For weeks at a time when Louise ceased to speak of her own accord, Marc relapsed into anxious ignorance, again losing all hope of Geneviève's return. His only consolation then lay in his daughter's presence beside him for a few hours on Thursdays and Sundays. On those days also it occasionally happened that the two chums of the Beaumont Training College, Joseph Simon and Sébastien Milhomme, arrived at the Maillebois school about three o'clock, and remained there until six, happy to meet their friend Louise, who like themselves was all aglow with youth and courage and faith. Their long chats were enlivened by merry laughter, which left some gaiety in the mournful home throughout the ensuing week. Marc, who felt comforted by these meetings, at times requested Joseph to bring his sister Sarah from the Lehmanns', and likewise told Sébastien that he would be happy to see his mother, Madame Alexandre, accompany him. The schoolmaster would have been delighted to gather a number of worthy folk, all the forces of the future, around him. At those affectionate meetings the sympathies of former times revived, acquiring a strength full of gentleness and gaiety, drawing Sébastien and Sarah, Joseph and Louise together; while the master, smiling and content to await victory at the hands of those who represented to-morrow, allowed good Mother Nature, beneficent love, to do their work.

All at once, amidst the disheartening delays of the Court of Cassation, at a moment when courage was forsaking David and Marc, they received a letter from Delbos acquainting them with some great news and requesting them to call on him. They did so in all haste. The great news—destined to burst on Beaumont like a thunderclap—was that, after a long and cruel struggle, Jacquin, the diocesan architect and foreman of the jury which had convicted Simon, had at last felt it absolutely necessary to relieve his conscience. Very pious, attending confession and Communion, strict in his faith, and in all respects an upright man, Jacquin had ended by feeling anxious with respect to his salvation, asking himself whether, as he was in possession of the truth, it was possible for him to keep silent any longer without incurring the risk of damnation. It was said that his confessor, feeling extremely perplexed, not daring to decide the question himself, had advised him to consult Father Crabot, and that if the architect had remained silent several months longer it was on account of the great pressure brought to bear on him by the Jesuit, who, in the name of the Church's political interests, had prevented him from speaking out. If, however, Jacquin was unable to keep his terrible secret any longer, it was precisely by reason of the anguish he felt as a Christian, one who believed that the Christ had descended upon earth to ensure the triumph of truth and justice. And the knowledge which consumed him was that of Judge Gragnon's illegal communication to the jury in the Simon case of a document unknown either to the prisoner or to his counsel. Summoned to the retiring room to enlighten the jurymen respecting the penalty which might attach to their verdict, the judge had shown them a letter received by him a moment previously, a letter from Simon to a friend, followed by a postscript and a paraph, which last was similar to the one on the copy-slip tendered as evidence. It was to this same letter and this paraph that Father Philibin had alluded in his sensational evidence; and now it had been established that if the body of the letter was indeed in Simon's handwriting, the postscript and the paraph were assuredly impudent forgeries, in fact gross ones, by which a child even would hardly have been deceived.

Thus David and Marc found Delbos triumphant: 'Ah! didn't I tell you so?' he exclaimed. 'That illegal communication is now proved! Jacquin has written to the President of the Court of Cassation, confessing the truth, and asking to be heard.... I knew that the letter was among the papers of the case, for Gragnon had not dared to destroy it. But how difficult it was to have it produced and submitted to the examination of experts! I scented a forgery; I felt that we were confronted by some more of the handiwork of that terrible Father Philibin! Ah! that man, how heavy and common he looked! But the more I fathom the affair the greater do his talents, his suppleness, artfulness, and audacity appear. He was not content with tearing off the stamped corner of the copy-slip, he also falsified one of Simon's letters, so arranging matters that this letter might prevail over the jury at the last moment. Yes, assuredly that forgery was his work!'

However, David, who had met with so many deceptions, retained some fears. 'But are you sure,' he asked, 'that Jacquin, who is the diocesan architect and at the mercy of the priests, will remain firm to the end?'

'Quite sure. You don't know Jacquin. He is not at the mercy of the priests; he is one of the few Christians who are governed solely by their consciences. Some extraordinary things have been told me respecting his interviews with Father Crabot. At first the Jesuit spoke in a domineering way, in the name of his imperative Deity, who forgives and even glorifies the worst deeds when the salvation of the Church is in question. But Jacquin answered back in the name of a good and equitable God, the God of the innocent and the just, who tolerates neither error, nor falsehood, nor crime. I wish I had been present; that battle between the mere believer and the political agent of a crumbling religion must have been a fine spectacle. However, I have been told that it was the Jesuit who ended by humbling himself, and entreating Jacquin, though he failed to prevent him from doing his duty——'

'All the same,' Marc interrupted, 'it took Jacquin a very long time to relieve his conscience.'

'Oh! no doubt; I don't say that his duty became manifest to him at once. For years, however, he did not know that President Gragnon's communication was illegal. Almost all jurors are similarly situated; they know nothing of the law, and take as correct whatever the chief magistrates may say to them. When Jacquin learnt the truth he hesitated evidently, and for years and years went about with a burden on his conscience, saying nothing, however, for fear of scandal. We shall never know the sufferings and the struggles of that man, who went regularly to confession and Communion, ever terrified by the thought that he was perhaps damning himself for all eternity. However, I can assure you that when he became certain that the document was a forgery, he no longer hesitated; he resolved to speak out, even if by doing so he should cause the cathedral of Saint Maxence to fall, for on no account was he disposed to disregard what he deemed to be his duty towards God.'

Then Delbos, like a man who, after long efforts, was at last reaching his goal, gaily summed up the situation, and David and Marc went off radiant with hope.

But how great was the commotion in Beaumont when Jacquin's letter to the Court of Cassation, his confession and his offer of evidence became known. Judge Gragnon hastily closed his doors, refusing to answer the journalists who applied to him, wrapping himself, as it were, in haughty silence. He was no longer a jovial, sarcastic sportsman and pursuer of pretty girls. People said that he was quite overwhelmed by the blow which had thus fallen on him on the eve of his retirement from the bench, at the moment when he was expecting to receive the collar of a Commandership in the Legion of Honour. Of recent years his wife, the once beautiful Madame Gragnon, having passed the age for reading poetry with General Jarousse's young officers, had decided to occupy herself in converting him, pointing out to him no doubt all the advantages of a pious old age; and he followed her to confession and Communion, giving a lofty example of fervent Catholicism, which explained the passionate zeal with which Father Crabot had tried to prevent Jacquin from relieving his conscience. The Jesuit, indeed, wished to save Gragnon, a believer of great importance and influence, of whom the Church was very proud.

Moreover, the whole judicial world of Beaumont sided with the presiding judge, defending the conviction and condemnation of Simon as its own work, its masterpiece, which none might touch without committing high treason against the country. Behind that fine assumption of indignation, however, there was base, shivering dread—dread of the galleys, dread lest the gendarmes should set their heavy hands some evening on the black or red robes, furred with ermine, whose wearers had imagined themselves to be above the laws. The handsome Raoul de La Bissonnière was no longer public prosecutor at Beaumont, he had been transferred to the neighbouring Appeal Court of Mornay, where he was growing embittered by his failure to secure a post in Paris, in spite of all his suppleness and skill under every succeeding government. On the other hand, Investigating Magistrate Daix had not quitted the town, where he had been promoted to the rank of counsellor; but he was still tortured by his terrible wife, whose ambition and craving for luxury made his home a hell. It was said that Daix, seized with remorse like Jacquin, was on the point of throwing off his wife's acrimonious authority, and relating how he had cowardly yielded to her representations, and sent Simon for trial, at the very moment when, from lack of proof, he was about to stay further proceedings. Thus the Palais de Justice was all agog, swept by gusts of fear and anger, pending the advent of the cataclysm which would at last annihilate the ancient worm-eaten framework of so-called human justice.

The political world of Beaumont was no less shaken, no less distracted. Lemarrois, the Deputy and Mayor, felt that the Radical Republican views he had long professed were losing their hold on the electorate, and that he might be swept away in this supreme crisis which was bringing the living strength of the people forward. Thus, in the much-frequented *salon* of his intelligent wife, the evolution towards reactionary courses became more pronounced. Among those now often seen there was Marcilly, once the representative of the intellectual young men, the hope of the French mind, but now reduced to a kind of political paralysis, bewildered by his inability to detect in which direction lay his personal interests, and forced to inaction by the haunting fear that if he should act in any particular way he might not be re-elected. Then another visitor was General Jarousse, who, though a mere cipher, now showed himself aggressive, spurred on, it seemed, by the perpetual nagging of his little, dusky, withered wife. And Prefect Hennebise also called at times, accompanied by the placid Madame Hennebise, each desiring to live at peace with everybody, such being indeed the wish of the government, whose motto was: 'No difficulties, only handshakes and smiles.' There was great fear of 'bad' elections, as the department was so enfevered by the revival of the Simon affair; and Marcilly and even Lemarrois, though they did not own it, had resolved to ally themselves secretly with Hector de Sanglebœuf and their other reactionary colleagues in order to overcome the Socialist candidates, particularly Delbos, whose success would become certain should he succeed in his efforts on behalf of the innocent prisoner.

All this tended to the confusion which broke out directly people heard of the intervention of Jacquin, by which the revision of the case was rendered inevitable. The Simonists triumphed, and for a few days the anti-Simonists seemed crushed. Nothing else was talked about on the aristocratic promenade of Les Jaffres; and though *Le Petit Beaumontais*, in order to inspirit its readers, declared every morning that the revision of the case would be refused by a majority of two to one, the friends of the Church remained plunged in desolation, for private estimates indicated quite a different result.

Meantime the delight shown among the University men was very temperate. Nearly all of them were Simonists, but they had hoped in vain so often that they now scarcely dared to rejoice. Rector Forbes was relieved to think that he would soon be rid of the case of that Maillebois schoolmaster, Marc Froment, about whom he was so frequently assailed by the reactionary forces. In spite of his desire to meddle with nothing, Forbes had been obliged to confer with Le Barazer respecting the necessity of an execution; and Le Barazer, whose own powers of resistance were exhausted, foresaw the moment when policy would compel him to sacrifice Marc. He had even mentioned it to Salvan, who had shown deep grief at the announcement. When, however, Marc came to him with the great news that made revision certain, the kind-hearted man revived to gaiety and gave his friend quite a triumphal greeting. He embraced him and then told him of the threatening danger from which the favourable decision of the Court of Cassation alone would save him.

'If revision should not be granted, my dear fellow,' he said, 'you would certainly be revoked, for this time you are deeply involved in the affair, and all the reactionaries demand your head.... However, the news you bring pleases me, for you are at last victorious, and our secular schools triumph.'

'They need to do so,' Marc replied; 'our conquests over error and ignorance are still so slight in spite of all your efforts to endow the region with good masters.'

'Certainly a good many lives will be needed; but, no matter, we are marching on, and we shall reach the goal,' Salvan responded with his usual gesture expressive of unshakable hope.

Perhaps the best proof that Marc was really victorious was found by him in the eager manner with which handsome Mauraisin, the Elementary Inspector, rushed towards him, that same day, just as he had quitted Salvan.

'Ah! my dear Monsieur Froment, I am very pleased to meet you,' the Inspector exclaimed. 'We see each other so seldom apart from the requirements of our duties.'

Since the revival of the affair, mortal anxiety had taken possession of Mauraisin, who at an earlier stage had openly sided with the anti-Simonists, convinced as he then was that the priests never allowed themselves to be beaten. But now, if they should lose the game, how would he be able to save himself? The idea of not being on the winning side distressed him greatly.

Though nobody was passing in the street, he leant towards Marc to whisper in his ear: 'For my part, you know, my dear Froment, I never doubted Simon's innocence. I was convinced of it at bottom. Only it is so necessary for public men like ourselves to remain prudent—is that not so?'

For a long time past Mauraisin had been keeping his eye on Salvan's post, hoping to secure it in due course; and in view of a possible triumph of the Simonists he felt it would be as well to side with them on the eve of victory. But as that victory was not yet quite certain he did not wish to exhibit himself in their company. So he speedily took leave of Marc, whispering, as he pressed his hand for the last time, 'Simon's triumph will be a triumph for all of us.'

On returning to Maillebois Marc perceived a change there also. Darras, the ex-Mayor, whom he chanced to meet, did not rest content with bowing to him discreetly, according to his wont, but stopped him in the middle of the high street, and talked and laughed with him for more than ten minutes. He, Darras, had been a Simonist at the outset, but since he had lost his position as Mayor he had put his flag in his pocket, and made it a habit to bolt his door before divulging what he thought. If, therefore, he now openly chatted with Marc, it must have been because Simon's acquittal seemed to him a certainty. As it happened, Philis, the new Mayor, went by at that moment, gliding swiftly over the pavement with his head bent and his eyes darting furtive glances around him. This amused Darras, who with a knowing look at Marc exclaimed: 'What pleases some displeases others, is it not so, Monsieur Froment? We all have our turns!'

Indeed a great change in public opinion gradually became manifest. Day by day for several weeks Marc observed the increasing favour of the cause he defended. However, the decisive importance of the success already achieved became most manifest to him when he received a letter from Baron Nathan, who was again staying at La Désirade, and who asked him to call there with respect to a prize for the Communal School, which he, the Baron, desired to found. Although Nathan, on two or three occasions previously, had given a hundred francs or so to be distributed in savings-bank deposits among the best pupils, Marc felt that the offer of a prize at that juncture was only a pretext. So he repaired to La Désirade full of wonder and curiosity.

He had not returned thither since the now distant day when he had accompanied David on his attempt to interest the all-powerful Baron in the cause of his accused and imprisoned brother. Marc remembered the most trifling details of that visit, the skilful manner in which the triumphant Jew, a king of finance and the father-in-law of a Sanglebœuf, had shaken off the poor Jew, on whom public execration had fallen. And now, on returning to La Désirade, Marc found that its majesty and beauty had increased. Recently a million of francs had been spent on new terraces and new fountains, which imparted an aspect of sovereign grandeur to the parterres in front of the château. Encompassed by plashing waters and a galaxy of marble nymphs, he ended by reaching the steps, where two tall lackeys, in liveries of green and gold, were waiting. On one of them conducting him to a little drawing-room, where he was requested to wait, he remained alone for a moment, and heard a confused murmur of voices in some neighbouring room. Then two doors were shut, all became quiet, and finally Baron Nathan entered with outstretched hand.

'Excuse me for having disturbed you, my dear Monsieur Froment,' he said, 'but I know how devoted you are to your pupils, and I wish to double the sum which I have been giving you of recent years. You are aware that my ideas are broad, that I desire to reward merit wherever it may be found, apart from all political and religious questions.... Yes, I make no difference between the congregational and the secular schools; I am for all France.'

Short and somewhat bent, with a yellow face, a bald cranium, and a large nose resembling the beak of a bird of prey, Nathan went on talking, while Marc gazed at him. The schoolmaster knew that of recent times the Baron had still further enriched himself by stealing a hundred millions of francs in a colonial affair, a deed of rapine, the huge booty of which he had been obliged to share with a Catholic bank. And he had now plunged into fierce reaction, for as new millions were added to his former ones he became more and more convinced that priests and soldiers were needed to enable him to retain his ill-gotten wealth. He was no longer content with having wormed his way, through his daughter, into the ancient family of the Sangleboeufs: he now absolutely denied his race, openly displaying a ferocious anti-Semitism, showing himself a monarchist, a militarist, a respectful friend of those who in olden time had burnt the Jews. Nevertheless—and this astonished Marc—Nathan, whatever his wealth, still retained much of his racial humility. A dread of the persecutions which had fallen on his ancestors appeared in his anxious eyes as they glanced at the doors as if he wished to be ready to slip under a table at the slightest sign of danger.

'So it is settled,' he said, after all sorts of involved explanations, 'and you will dispose of these two hundred francs yourself, as you please, for I have perfect confidence in your sagacity.'

Marc thanked him, but still failed to understand the meaning of it all. Even a politic desire to remain on good terms with everybody, a wish to be among the Simonists if they should win the battle, did not explain that flattering and useless appointment, that over-cordial reception at La

Désirade. However, just as the schoolmaster was retiring, there came an explanation.

Baron Nathan, having accompanied him to the drawing-room door, detained him there, and with a keen smile, which seemed prompted by a sudden inspiration, exclaimed: 'My dear Monsieur Froment, I am going to be very indiscreet.... When I was informed of your arrival just now, I happened to be with somebody, an important personage, who exclaimed, "Monsieur Froment! Oh! I should be so pleased to have a moment's conversation with him!" A cry from the heart in fact.'

The Baron paused, waiting a few seconds in the hope that he would be questioned. Then, as Marc remained silent, he laughed and said in a jesting way: 'You would be greatly surprised if I told you who the personage was.' And as the schoolmaster still looked grave, remaining on the defensive, Nathan blurted out everything: 'It was Father Crabot. You did not expect that, eh?... But he came to lunch here this morning. As you may know, he honours my daughter with his affection, and is a frequent visitor here. Well, he expressed to me a desire to have some conversation with you. Setting aside all matters of opinion, he is a man of the rarest merit. Why should you refuse to see him?'

To this Marc, who at last understood the object of the appointment given him, and whose curiosity was more and more aroused, quietly responded: 'But I don't refuse to see Father Crabot. If he has anything to say to me I will listen to him willingly.'

'Very good, very good!' exclaimed the Baron, delighted with the success of his diplomacy. 'I will go to tell him.'

Again the two doors opened, one after the other, and a confused murmur of voices once more reached the little drawing-room. Then all relapsed into silence, and Marc was left waiting for some time. Having at last drawn near to the window he saw the persons, whose voices he had heard, step on to the adjoining terrace. And he recognised Hector de Sangleboeuf and his wife, the still beautiful Léa, accompanied by their good friend, the Marchioness de Boise, who, though her fifty-seventh birthday was now past, remained a buxom blonde, the ruins of whose beauty were magnificent. Nathan likewise appeared, and one could also divine that Father Crabot was standing at the glass door of the grand drawing-room, still talking to his hosts, who left him in possession of the apartment in order that he might receive the visitor as if he were at home.

The Marchioness de Boise seemed particularly amused by the incident. Though she had originally resolved to disappear as soon as she should be fifty, unwilling as she was to impose too old a mistress on Hector, she had ended by making the château her permanent home. Besides, people said that she was still adorable, so why should she not continue to ensure the happiness of the husband whose marriage she had so wisely negotiated, and of the wife whose tender friend she was? Thus age might come but happiness still reigned at La Désirade, amid its luxurious appointments and Father Crabot's discreet smiles and pious benisons.

As Marc looked out of the window and observed the terrible Sanglebœuf waving his arms and shaking his carroty head, it seemed to him that this clerical champion with the heavy face and the narrow, stubborn brow was deploring the practice of so much diplomacy, the honour which Father Crabot accorded to a petty anarchical schoolmaster by thus receiving him. Sanglebœuf had never once fought in his cuirassier days, but he always talked of sabring people. Although the Marchioness, after securing his election as a deputy, had made him rally to the Republic—in accordance with the Pope's express commands—he still and ever prated about his regiment, and flew into a passion whenever there was any question of the flag. Indeed, he would have committed blunder upon blunder had it not been for that intelligent Marchioness, and this was one of the reasons she gave for remaining near him, Again, on this occasion, she had to intervene and lead him and his wife away, walking slowly between them, in the direction of the park, and showing the while much gaiety of mien, and motherliness of manner towards both.

Baron Nathan, however, had quickly returned to the grand drawing-room, the glass door of which he closed; and almost immediately afterwards Marc heard himself called:

'Kindly follow me, my dear Monsieur Froment.'

The Baron led him through a billiard-room; then, having opened the drawing-room door, drew back and ushered him in, delighted, it seemed, with the strange part he was playing, his body bowed in a posture which again showed racial humility reviving in the triumphant king of finance.

'Please enter—you are awaited.'

Nathan himself did not enter, but discreetly closed the door and disappeared; while Marc, amazed, found himself in the presence of Father Crabot, who stood, in his long black gown, in the centre of the spacious and sumptuous room, hung with crimson and gold. A moment's silence followed.

The Jesuit, whose noble mien, whose lofty and elegant carriage Marc well remembered, seemed to him to have greatly aged. His hair had whitened, and his countenance was ravaged by all the terrible anxiety he had experienced for some time past. But the caressing charm of his voice, its grave and captivating modulations, had remained.

'As circumstances have brought us both to this friendly house, monsieur,' said he, 'you will perhaps excuse me for having prompted an interview which I have long desired. I am aware of your merits, I can render homage to all convictions, when they are sincere, loyal, and courageous.'

He went on speaking in this strain for some minutes, heaping praises on his adversary as if to daze him and win him over. But the device was too familiar and too childish to influence Marc, who, after bowing politely, quietly awaited the rest, striving even to conceal his curiosity, for only some very grave reason could have induced such a man as Father Crabot to run the risk of such an interview.

'How deplorable it is,' the Jesuit at last exclaimed, 'that the misfortunes of the times should separate minds so fit to understand each other! Some of the victims of our dissensions are really to be pitied. For instance, there is President Gragnon— —'

Then, as a hasty gesture escaped the schoolmaster, he broke off in order to interpolate a brief explanation. 'I name him,' he said, 'because I know him well. He is a penitent of mine—a friend. A loftier soul, a more upright and loyal heart could be found nowhere. You are aware of the frightful position in which he finds himself—that charge of prevarication,[2] which means the collapse of his entire judicial career. He no longer sleeps; you would pity him if you were to witness his sufferings.'

> [2] The word 'Prevarication' is used in a legal sense, as signifying the betrayal of the interests of one party in a lawsuit by collusion with the other party. The French call this *forfaiture.—Trans.*

At last Marc understood everything. They wished to save Gragnon, who only yesterday had been an all-powerful son of the Church, which felt it would be grievously maimed if he should be struck down.

'I can understand his torment,' Marc finally answered, 'but he is paying the penalty of his transgression. A judge must know the laws, and the illegal communication of which he was guilty had frightful consequences.'

'No, no, I assure you, he acted in all simplicity,' the Jesuit exclaimed. 'That letter which he received at the last moment seemed to him without importance. He still had it in his hand when he was summoned to the jurymen's retiring room, and he no longer remembers how it happened that he showed it to them.'

Marc gave a little shrug of the shoulders. 'Well,' he responded, 'he will only have to tell that to the new judges, if there should be a new trial.... In any case I hardly understand your intervention with me. I can do nothing.'

'Oh! do not say that, monsieur! We know how great your power is, however modest your position may seem to be. And that is why I thought of applying to you. Throughout this affair all thought and action and willpower have been centred in you. You are the friend of the Simon family, which will do whatever you advise. So, come, will you not spare an unfortunate man, whose ruin is by no means indispensable for your cause?'

Father Crabot joined his hands and entreated his adversary so fervently that the latter, again all astonishment, wondered what could be the real reason of such a desperate appeal, such clumsy and impolitic insistence. Did the Jesuit feel that the cause he defended was lost? Did he possess private information which made him regard revision as a certainty? In any case, matters had come to such a pass, that he was now ready to leave something to the fire in order to save the rest. He abandoned his former creatures, who were now too deeply compromised. That poor Brother Fulgence had a befogged, unbalanced mind, spoilt by excessive pride; disastrous consequences had attended his actions. That unfortunate Father Philibin had always been full of faith, no doubt; but then there were many gaps in his nature. He was deplorably deficient in moral sense. As for the disastrous Brother Gorgias, Father Crabot cast him off entirely; he was one of those adventurous, erring sons of the Church, who become its curse. And if the Jesuit did not go so far as to admit the possible innocence of Simon, he was, at least, not far from believing Brother Gorgias capable of every crime.

'You see, my dear sir,' he said, 'I do not deceive myself; but there are other men whom it would be really cruel to visit too severely for mere errors. Help us to save them, and we will requite the service by ceasing to contend with you in other matters.'

Never had Marc so plainly realised his strength, the very strength of truth. He answered, engaging in quite a long discussion, desirous as he was of forming a final opinion with respect to the merits of Father Crabot. And his stupefaction increased as he fathomed the extraordinary poverty of argument, the arrant clumsiness too, which accompanied the vanity of this man, accustomed never to be contradicted. Was this, then, the profound diplomatist whose crafty genius was feared by everybody, and the presence of whose hand was suspected in every incident, as if, indeed, he ruled the world? In this interview, which had been prepared so clumsily, he showed himself a poor bewildered individual, committing himself far more than was necessary, even incompetent to defend his faith against one who was merely possessed of sense and logic. A mediocrity—that was what he was—a mediocrity, with a *façade* of social gifts, which imposed on the man in the street. His real strength lay in the stupidity of his flock, the submissiveness with which the faithful bent low before his statements, which they regarded as being beyond discussion. And Marc ended by understanding that he was confronted by a mere show Jesuit, one of those who for decorative purposes were allowed by their Order to thrust themselves forward, shine, and charm, while, in the rear, other Jesuits—such, for instance, as Father Poirier, the Provincial installed at Rozan, whose name was never mentioned—directed everything like unknown sovereign rulers hidden away in distant places of retreat.

Father Crabot, however, was shrewd enough to understand at last that he was taking the wrong course with Marc, and he thereupon did what he could to recover his lost ground. The whole ended by an exchange of frigid courtesies. Then Baron Nathan, who must have remained listening outside the door, reappeared, looking also very discomfited, with only one remaining anxiety, which was to rid La Désirade as soon as possible of the presence of that petty schoolmaster, who was such a fool that he could not even understand his own interests. He escorted him to the terrace and watched his departure. And Marc, as he went his way among the parterres, the plashing waters, and the marble nymphs, again caught a glimpse of the Marchioness de Boise, laughing affectionately with her good friends Hector and Léa, as all three strolled slowly under the far-spreading foliage.

On the evening of that same day Marc repaired to the Rue du Trou, having given David an appointment at the Lehmanns'. He found them all in a state of delirious joy, for a telegram from a friend in Paris had just informed them that the Court of Cassation had at last pronounced an unanimous judgment, quashing the proceedings of Beaumont, and sending Simon before the Assize Court of Rozan. For Marc this news was like a flash of light, and what he had regarded as Father Crabot's folly seemed to him more excusable than before. The Jesuit had evidently been well informed; that judgment had been known to him; and, revision becoming a certainty, he had simply wished to save those whom he thought might still be saved. And now, at the Lehmanns', all were weeping with joy, for the long calamity was over. Wildly did Joseph and Sarah kiss Rachel, their poor, aged, and exhausted mother. Both children and wife were intoxicated by the thought of the return of the father, the husband, for whom they had mourned and longed so much. Outrage and torture were all forgotten, for acquittal was now certain; nobody doubted it either at Maillebois or at Beaumont. And David and Marc, those two brave workers in the cause of justice, also embraced each other, drawn together by a great impulse of affection and hope.

But, as the days went by, anxiety arose once more. At the penal settlement yonder Simon had fallen so dangerously ill that for a long time yet it would be impossible to bring him back to France. Months and months might elapse before the new trial would begin at Rozan. And thus all necessary time was given to the spirit of injustice to revive and spread once more in the midst of mendacity and the multitude's cowardly ignorance.

CHAPTER III

During the year which followed, a year full of anxiety, uneasiness, and contention, the Church made a supreme effort to regain her power. Never had her position been more critical, more threatened, than during that desperate battle, by which the duration of her empire might be prolonged for a century, or perhaps two centuries, should she win it. In order to do so it was necessary she should continue to educate and train the youth of France, retain her sway over children and women, and avail herself of the ignorance of the humble in such wise as to mould them and make them all error, credulity, and submissiveness, even as she needed them to be in order to reign. The day when she might be forbidden to teach, when her schools would be closed, and disappear, would prove for her the beginning of the end, when she would be annihilated amidst a new and free people, which would have grown up outside the pale of her falsehoods, cultivating an ideal of reason and humanity. And the hour was a grave one. That Simon affair, with the expected return and triumph of the innocent prisoner, might deal a most terrible blow to the Congregational schools by glorifying the secular ones. Meantime Father Crabot, who wished to save Judge Gragnon, was so compromised himself that he had disappeared from society and hidden himself, pale and trembling, in his lonely cell. Father Philibin, who had been consigned to an Italian convent, was spending the remainder of his days in penitence, unless indeed he were already dead. Brother Fulgence, removed by his superiors in punishment for the discredit which had fallen on his school, a third of whose pupils had already quitted it, was said to have fallen dangerously ill in the distant department whither he had been sent. Finally, Brother Gorgias had fled, fearing that he might be arrested, and feeling that his principals were forsaking him, willing to sacrifice him as an expiatory victim. And this flight had increased the anxiety of the defenders of the Church, who lived only with the thought of fighting a last and merciless battle when the Simon affair should come before the Rozan Assize Court.

Marc also, while lamenting Simon's ill health, which delayed his return to France, was preparing for that same battle, fully realising its decisive importance. Almost every Thursday, sometimes with David, sometimes alone, he repaired to Beaumont, calling first on Delbos, to whom he made suggestions, and whom he questioned about the slightest incidents of the week. And afterwards he went to see Salvan, who kept him informed of the

state of public opinion, every fluctuation of which set all classes in the town agog. In this wise, then, one Thursday, Marc paid a visit to the Training College, and on quitting it went down the Avenue des Jaffres, where, close to the cathedral of St. Maxence, he was upset by a most unexpected meeting.

On one of the deserted sidewalks of the avenue, at a spot where scarcely anybody was ever seen after four o'clock, he perceived Geneviève seated on a bench, and looking very downcast, weary, and lonely in the cold shadow falling from the cathedral, whose proximity encouraged the moss to grow on the trunks of the old elms.

For a moment Marc remained motionless, quite thunderstruck. He had met his wife in Maillebois at long intervals, but invariably in the company of Madame Duparque; and on those occasions she had passed through the streets with absent-minded eyes, on her way, no doubt, to some devotional exercise. This time, however, they found themselves face to face, in perfect solitude, parted by none. Geneviève had seen him, and was looking at him with an expression in which he fancied he could detect great suffering, and an unacknowledged craving for help. Thus he went forward, and even ventured to seat himself on the same bench, though at some little distance from her, for fear lest he should frighten her and drive her away.

Deep silence reigned. It was June, and the sun, descending towards the horizon in a vast stretch of limpid sky, transpierced the surrounding foliage with slender golden darts; while little wandering zephyrs already began to cool the warm afternoon atmosphere. And Marc still looked at his wife, saying nothing, but feeling deeply moved as he noticed that she had grown thinner and paler, as if after a serious illness. Her face, crowned by splendid fair hair, and with large eyes which once had been all passion and gaiety, had not only become emaciated, but had acquired an expression of ardent anxiety, the torment of a parching thirst, which nothing could assuage. Her eyelids quivered, and two tears, which she vainly tried to force back, coursed down her cheeks. Then Marc began to speak—in such a way that it seemed as if he had quitted her only the previous day, such indeed was his desire to reassure her.

'Is our little Clément well?' he asked.

She did not answer immediately, for she feared, no doubt, that she might reveal the emotion which was choking her. The little boy, who had lately completed his fourth year, was no longer at Dherbecourt. Having removed him from his nurse, Geneviève now kept him with her in spite of all her grandmother's scoldings.

'He is quite well,' she said at last in a slightly tremulous voice, though on her side also she strove to affect a kind of indifferent quietude.

'And our Louise,' Marc resumed, 'are you satisfied with her?'

'Yes: she does not comply with my desires; you have remained the master of her mind; but she is well behaved, she studies, and I do not complain of her.'

Silence fell again, embarrassment once more stayed their tongues. That allusion to their daughter's first Communion, and the terrible quarrel which had parted them, had been sufficient. Yet the virulence of that quarrel was necessarily abating day by day, the girl herself having assumed all responsibility by her quiet resolve to await her twentieth year before making any formal confession of religious faith. In her gentle way she had exhausted her mother's resolution; and indeed a gesture of lassitude had escaped the latter when speaking of her, as if she had referred to some long-desired happiness, all hope of which had fled. A few moments went by, and then Marc gently ventured to put another question to her: 'And you, my friend, you have been so ill: how are you now?'

She shrugged her shoulders in a hopeless way, and was again obliged to force back her tears. 'I? Oh, I have long ceased to know how I am! But no matter, I resign myself to live since God gives me the strength to do so.'

So great was Marc's distress, so deeply was his whole being stirred by a quiver of loving compassion at the sight of such great suffering, that a cry of intense anxiety sprang from his lips: 'Geneviève, my Geneviève, what ails you? what is your torment? Tell me! Ah, if I could only console you, and cure you!'

Thus speaking, he came nearer to her on the bench, near enough indeed to touch the folds of her gown, but she hastily drew back. 'No, no, we have nothing more in common,' she exclaimed. 'You can no longer do anything for me, my friend, for we belong to different worlds.... Ah! if I were to tell you! But of what use would it be? You would not understand me!'

Nevertheless, she went on speaking; and in short and feverish sentences, never noticing that she was confessing herself, she told him of her torture, her daily increasing anguish, for she had reached one of those distressful hours when the heart instinctively opens and overflows. She related how, unknown to Madame Duparque, she had escaped that afternoon from Maillebois, in order to speak with a famous missionary, Father Athanase, whose pious counsels were at that time revolutionising the pious folk of Beaumont. The missionary was merely sojourning there for a short time, but it was said that he had already worked some marvellous cures—a blessing, a prayer, from his lips having restored angelic calmness to the unappeasable souls of women who were racked by their yearning for Jesus. And Geneviève had just left the neighbouring cathedral, where for two hours she had remained in prayer, after confessing to that holy man her unquenchable thirst for divine happiness. But he had merely absolved her for what he called excess of pride and human passion, and by way of penitence had told her to occupy her mind with humble duties, such as the care of the poor and the sick. In vain afterwards had she striven to humble, annihilate herself, in the darkest, the loneliest chapel of St. Maxence; she had not found peace, she had not satisfied her hunger; she still glowed with the same craving—a return for the gift of her whole being to the Deity, that gift which she had tendered again and again, though never once had it brought real peace and happiness to her flesh and her heart.

As Marc listened to what she said, he began to suspect the truth, and whatever might be his sadness at seeing his Geneviève so wretched, a quiver of hope arose within him. Plainly enough, neither Abbé Quandieu nor even Father Théodose had satisfied the intense need of love that existed in her nature. She had known love, and she must still love the man, the husband, whom she had quitted, and who adored her. Mere mystical delights had left her unsatisfied and irritated. She was now but the proud, stubborn daughter of Catholicism, who turns desperately to harsher and more frantic religious practices, as to stronger stupefacients, in order to numb the bitterness and rebellion induced by increasing disillusion. Everything pointed to it: the revival of motherliness in her nature, for she had taken little Clément back, and busied herself with him, and she even found some consolation in Louise, who exercised a gentle healing influence over her, leading her back a little more each day towards the father, the husband. Then, also, there were her dissensions with her terrible grandmother, and her dawning dislike for the little house on the Place des Capucins, where she at last felt she could no longer live, for its coldness, silence, and gloom were deathly. And, after failing with Abbé Quandieu and Father Théodose, her sufferings had led her to make a supreme attempt with that powerful missionary, to whom she had transferred her faith, that miracle-working confessor, whom she had hastened to consult in secret for fear lest she might be prevented, and who, by way of relief, had only been able to prescribe practices which, in the circumstances, were childish.

'But, my Geneviève,' Marc cried again, carried away, losing all thought of prudence, 'if you are thus beset, thus tortured, it is because you lack our home! You are too unhappy: come back, come back, I entreat you!'

Her pride bristled up, however, and she answered: 'No, no, I shall never go back to you. I am not unhappy: it is untrue. I am punished for having loved you, for having been part of you, for having had a share in your crime. Grandmother does right to remind me of it when I am so weak as to complain. I expiate your sin, God strikes me to punish you, and it is your poison which burns me beyond hope of relief.'

'But, my poor wife, all that is monstrous. They are driving you mad! If it is true that I set a new harvest in you, it is precisely on that harvest that I rely to ensure our happiness some day. Yes, we became so blended one with the other that we can never be wholly parted. And you will end by returning to me: our children will bring you back. The pretended poison which your foolish grandmother talks about is our love itself; it is working in your heart, and it will bring you back.'

'Never!... God would strike us down, both of us,' she retorted. 'You drove me from our home by your blasphemy. If you had really loved me, you would not have taken my daughter from me, by refusing to let her make her first Communion. How can I return to a home of impiety where it would not even be allowable for me to pray? Ah! how wretched I am; nobody, nobody loves me, and heaven itself will not open!'

She burst into sobs. Filled with despair by that frightful cry of distress Marc felt that it would be useless and cruel to torture her further. The hour for reunion had not yet come. Silence fell between them once more, while in the distance, on the Avenue des Jaffres, the cries of some children at play rose into the limpid evening atmosphere.

During their impassioned converse they had at last drawn nearer to each other on the lonely bench; and now, seated side by side, they seemed to be reflecting, their glances wandering away amid the golden dust of the sunset. At last Marc spoke again, as if finishing his thoughts aloud: 'I do not think, my friend, that you gave for a moment any credit to the abominable charges with which certain people wished to besmirch me *à propos* of my brotherly intercourse with Mademoiselle Mazeline.'

'Oh! no,' Geneviève answered quickly, 'I know you, and I know her. Do not imagine that I have become so foolish as to believe all that has been said to me.'

Then with some slight embarrassment she continued: 'It is the same with me. Some people, I know it, have set me among the flock which Father Théodose is said to have turned into a kind of *cour galante*. In the first place I do not admit that anything of the kind exists. Father Théodose is, perhaps, rather too proud of his person, but I believe his faith to be sincere. Besides, I should have known how to defend myself—you do not doubt it, I hope?'

In spite of his sorrow Marc could not help smiling slightly. Geneviève's evident embarrassment indicated that there had been some audacity on the part of the Capuchin, and that she had checked it. Assuming this to be the case Marc felt the better able to understand why she was so perturbed and embittered.

'I certainly do not doubt it,' he responded. 'I know you, as you know me, and I am aware that you are incapable of wrong-doing. I have no anxiety respecting Father Théodose on your account, whatever another husband of my acquaintance may have to say.... Yet all the same I regret that you were so badly advised as to quit worthy Abbé Quandieu for that handsome monk.'

A fugitive blush which appeared on Geneviève's cheeks while her husband was speaking told him that he had guessed aright. It was not without a profound knowledge of woman in her earlier years, when an *amorosa* may exist within the penitent, that Father Crabot had advised Madame Duparque to remove her daughter from the charge of old Abbé Quandieu and place her in that of handsome Father Théodose. The Catholic doctors are well aware that love alone can kill love, and that a woman who loves apart from Christ never wholly belongs to Christ. The return of Geneviève to her husband and her sin was fatal unless she should cease to love, or rather unless she should love elsewhere. But, as it happened, Father Théodose was not expert in analysing human nature, he had blundered with respect to the passionate yet loyal penitent confided to his hands, and had thus precipitated the crisis, provoking repugnance and rebellion in that distracted, suffering woman, who, without as yet returning to sober reason, saw the glorious, mystical stage-scenery of the religion of her childhood collapse around her.

Well pleased with the symptoms which he fancied he could detect, Marc asked somewhat maliciously: 'And so Father Théodose is no longer your confessor?'

Geneviève turned her clear eyes upon him, and answered plainly: 'No, Father Théodose does not suit me, and I have gone back to Abbé Quandieu, who, as grandmother rightly says, lacks warmth, but who quiets me at times, for he is very kind.'

For a moment she seemed to ponder. Then, in an undertone, she allowed another avowal to cross her lips: 'All the same, the dear man does not know how greatly he has increased the torment in which I live by what he said to me about that abominable affair——'

She stopped short, and Marc, guessing the truth, becoming quite impassioned now that this subject was broached, continued: 'The Simon affair, eh? Abbé Quandieu believes Simon to be innocent, does he not?'

Geneviève had cast her eyes towards the ground. For a moment she remained silent; then said, very faintly: 'Yes, he believes in his innocence; he told me so with great mystery in the choir of his church, at the foot of the altar, before our Lord who heard him.'

'And you yourself, Geneviève, tell me, do you now believe in Simon's innocence?'

'No, I do not, I cannot. You must remember that I should never have left you had I believed him innocent, for his innocence would have meant the guilt of the defenders of God. You, by defending him, charged God with error and falsehood.'

Marc well remembered the circumstances. He again saw his wife bring him the news of the revision, growing exasperated at the sight of his delight, exclaiming that there was no truth or justice outside heaven, and at last fleeing from the house where her faith was outraged. And now that she seemed to him to be shaken he desired more ardently than ever to convince her of the truth, for he felt that he would win her back as soon as with the triumph of truth her mind should awaken to the necessity of justice.

'But once more, Geneviève, my Geneviève, it is impossible that you, who are so upright and so sincere, whose mind is so clear when the superstitions of your childhood do not cloud it—it is impossible that you should believe such gross falsehoods. Inform yourself, read the documents.'

'But I am fully informed, I assure you, my friend; I have read everything.'

'You have read all the documents which have been published? All the inquiry of the Court of Cassation?'

'Why, yes! I have read everything that has appeared in *Le Petit Beaumontais*. You know very well that grandmother takes that paper every morning.'

With a violent gesture Marc gave expression to his disgust and indignation. 'Ah well, my darling, you are, indeed, fully informed! The vile print you speak of is a sewer of poison, which disseminates only filth and falsehood. Documents are falsified in it, texts are mutilated, and the poor credulous minds of the poor and the lowly are gorged with stupid fables. [1] ... You are simply poisoned like many other worthy folk.'

[1] This is exactly what happened in the Dreyfus case. If, apart from all those who, hating Dreyfus as a Jew, were resolved *a priori* to regard him as guilty whatever might be the evidence, there are still millions of Frenchmen who honestly retain a belief in his culpability, this is because

scores of French newspapers—those owned or patronised by the Nationalist party and the Roman Catholic Church—deliberately falsified and mutilated documents and evidence, serving to their readers only such particulars as tended to indicate the prisoner's guilt. It is hardly too much to say that half of France is still ignorant of the real facts of the Dreyfus case. We are often told that the press has much power for good: never was its power for evil more strikingly exemplified than in that lamentable affair, from the effects of which France is still suffering.—*Trans.*

She herself, no doubt, was conscious that the folly and impudence of *Le Petit Beaumontais* were excessive, for again she cast down her eyes, and looked distressed.

'Listen!' Marc resumed. 'Let me send you the complete verbatim report of the Court's inquiry, with the documents annexed to it; and promise me that you will read everything attentively and straightforwardly.'

But at this suggestion she vivaciously raised her head: 'No, no; send me nothing. I do not wish it.'

'Why?'

'Because it is useless. There is no need for me to read anything.'

He looked at her, again feeling discouraged and grieved.

'Say rather that you won't read.'

'Well, yes, if you prefer it that way, I won't read anything. As grandmother says: "What is the use of it?" Ought one not always to distrust one's reason?'

'You won't read anything because you fear you might be convinced, because you already doubt the things which, only yesterday, you regarded as certainties.'

She interrupted him with a gesture of fatigue and unconcern, but he continued: 'And the words of Abbé Quandieu pursue you; you ask yourself with terror how a holy priest can believe in an innocence which, if recognised, would compel you to curse all the years of error with which you have tortured our poor home.'

This time she did not even make a gesture, but it was apparent that she had resolved to listen no further. For a moment her glance remained fixed on the ground. Then she slowly said: 'Do not amuse yourself by increasing my sorrow. Our life has been shattered. It is all over. I should deem myself still more guilty than now if I were to go back to you. And what personal relief could it give you to imagine that I made a mistake, and that I have not found my grandmother's house to be the home of peace and faith in which I thought I was taking refuge? My sufferings would not cure yours.'

This, as Marc felt, was almost a confession—an acknowledgment of her secret regret at having quitted him, and of the anxious doubts into which she had sunk. Once more, therefore, he exclaimed: 'But if you are unhappy, say it! And come back; bring the children with you; the house still awaits you! It would be great joy, great happiness.'

But she stood up and repeated, like one who obstinately remains blind and deaf: 'I am not unhappy. I am being punished, and I will endure my punishment to the end. And if you have any pity for me, remain here; do not try to follow me. Should you meet me again, too, turn your head away, for all is ended, all must be ended, between us.'

Then she went off along the deserted avenue, amid the paling gold of the sunset, her figure quite sombre, tall, and slim; and all that Marc could still see of her beauty was her splendid fair hair, which a last sunbeam irradiated. He obediently refrained from moving, but, hoping for a last glance of farewell, he watched her as she walked away. She did not turn, however; she disappeared from view among the trees, while the evening wind, now rising, passed with a chilling quiver beneath the foliage.

When Marc painfully rose to his feet, he was amazed to see his good friend Salvan standing before him, with a happy smile on his lips. 'Ah! my fine lover, so this is how I catch you giving assignations in lonely corners! I saw you already some time ago, but remained watching, for I did not wish to disturb you.... So this is why you remained with me such a short time when you called at the college this afternoon, Master Slyboots!'

Sadly shaking his head, Marc walked away beside his old friend. 'No, no,' he said, 'we merely met by chance, and my heart is quite lacerated.'

Then he recounted the meeting, and the long conversation from which he had just emerged feeling more convinced than ever that the rupture was definitive. Salvan, who had never consoled himself for having promoted a marriage which, however happy at the outset, was ending so badly, and who recognised that he had acted with great imprudence in wedding free thought to the Church, listened attentively, ceasing to smile, yet looking fairly satisfied.

'But that is not so bad,' he said at last. 'You surely did not expect that our poor Geneviève would throw herself at your head, and entreat you to take her back? When a woman leaves her husband to give herself to God, as your wife did, her pride prevents her from acknowledging in that way the distress she now feels at having failed to find the contentment she anticipated. None the less, in my opinion, Geneviève is passing through a frightful crisis, which may bring her back to you at any moment.... If truth should enlighten her, she will act at once. She has retained too much sense to be unjust.'

And again becoming gay and animated, Salvan went on: 'I never told you, my friend, of the attempts I made with Madame Duparque of recent years. As they resulted in nothing, there was no occasion for me to vaunt them to you. However, when your wife acted so inconsiderately, when she left you, I thought of giving her a little lecture, for I was an old friend of her father's, and, besides, I had been her own guardian. That circumstance naturally gave me admittance to the dismal little house on the Place des Capucins. But you can have no idea of the ferocious manner in which the terrible old grandmother received me. She would not leave me alone with Geneviève for a moment, and she interrupted every conciliatory phrase of mine with imprecations intended to fall on you. Nevertheless, I think I managed to say what I wished to say. True, the poor child was in no fit state to listen to me. When Catholic training revives, the ravages which religious exaltation may cause in a woman's brain are frightful. Geneviève, for her part, appeared well-balanced and healthy when you married her; but that unfortunate Simon affair sufficed to shatter all equilibrium. She would not even listen to me; her answers were so wild and foolish as to make one's reason stagger. Briefly, I was beaten. I was not exactly turned out of doors, but, after two subsequent attempts made at long intervals, I lost all hope of introducing a little reasonableness into that abode of insanity, where poor Madame Berthereau, in spite of her sufferings, seemed the only person who retained a little good sense.'

'You see very well that there is no hope,' responded Marc, who remained very gloomy. 'One cannot reclaim people when they so stubbornly persist in refusing to make themselves acquainted with the truth.'

'Why not?' asked Salvan. 'I'm done for, that's true. It would be useless for me to make any fresh attempt; they would stop up their eyes and ears beforehand in order to see and hear nothing. But remember that you have the most powerful of helpers, the best of advocates, the shrewdest of diplomatists, the most skilful of captains, and in fact the most triumphant of conquerors at work in that house!'

He laughed, and, growing quite excited, resumed: 'Yes, yes, your charming Louise, whom I'm very fond of, and whom I regard as a prodigy of good sense and grace. The firm and yet gentle behaviour of that young girl, ever since her twelfth year, has been that of a heroine. I know of no loftier or more touching example. Seldom does one meet with such precocious sense and courage. And she is all deference and affection, even when she refuses to do what her mother desires, by reason of her promise to you respecting her first Communion. Now that she has acquired the right to keep that promise, you should see how prettily, how sedately, she manœuvres to effect the conquest of that house where everybody is against her. Even her grandmother becomes tired of scolding. But her dexterity is most marvellous with her mother, whom she encompasses with an active worship, with all sorts of attentions, as if dealing with some convalescent patient whose physical and moral strength must first of all be restored, in order that she may afterwards return to ordinary life. She seldom speaks to her mother of you, but she accustoms her to live in an atmosphere which is full of you, full of your thoughts and your love. She is there like your other self, never pausing in her endeavours to bring about the return of the wife and mother, by reconnecting the severed bond with her own caressing hands. And if your wife returns to you, my friend, it will be the child who will bring her back, the all-powerful child, whose presence ensures health and peace in one's home.'

Marc listened, feeling deeply moved, and reviving to hope. 'Ah! may it be true,' said he; 'nevertheless my poor Geneviève is still very ill.'

'Let your little healer do her work,' Salvan responded: 'the kiss she gives her mother every morning brings life with it.... If Geneviève suffers such torture it is because life is struggling within her, and wresting her a little more each day from the deadly crisis in which you nearly lost her. As soon as good Mother Nature triumphs over mystical imbecility, she and your children will be in your arms.... Come, my friend, be brave. It would be hard indeed if, after restoring poor Simon to his family, your own domestic happiness should not be assured by the triumph of truth and justice.'

They shook hands in brotherly fashion, and Marc, who returned to Maillebois somewhat comforted, found himself on the morrow in the thick of the fight again. The flight of Brother Gorgias had had a disastrous effect in the little town, and the great days of the affair were now beginning afresh. There was not a house whose inmates did not quarrel and fight over the possible guilt of that terrible Christian Brother, who, in disappearing from the scene, had impudently written to *Le Petit Beaumontais* to explain that, as his cowardly superiors had decided to abandon him to his enemies, he was about to place himself in safety, in order that he might be free to defend himself when and how he pleased.

A much more important feature of this letter was, however, a revised statement which Gorgias made in it to account for the presence of the famous copy-slip in the paper gag found near Zéphirin's body. No doubt the complicated story of a forgery, invented by his leaders, who were unwilling even to admit that the copy-slip had come from the Brothers' school, had always been regarded by Gorgias as idiotic. He must have thought it stupid to deny the origin of the slip and the authenticity of the initialling. Although every expert in the world might ascribe that initialling to Simon, it would remain his, Gorgias's, handiwork in the estimation of all honest and sensible folk. However, as his superiors had threatened to abandon him to his own resources if he did not accept their version of the affair, he had resigned himself and relinquished his own. It was to the latter that he now reverted, for since the missing corner bearing the school stamp had been found at Father Philibin's, he regarded his superiors' version as utterly ridiculous. It seemed to him absurd to pretend, as the Congregations did, that Simon had procured a stamp, or had caused one to be made, with the deliberate intention of ruining the Brothers' school. Now, therefore, realising that his supporters were on the point of forsaking and sacrificing him, Gorgias left them of his own accord, and by way of intimidation revealed a part of the truth. His new version, which upset all the credulous readers of *Le Petit Beaumontais*, was that the copy-slip had really come from the Brothers', and had been initialled by himself, but that Zéphirin had assuredly taken it home with him from the school, even as Victor Milhomme had taken a similar slip, in spite of all prohibitions; and that Simon had thus found it on the table in his victim's room on the night of the abominable crime.

A fortnight after the appearance of this version the newspaper published a fresh letter from Brother Gorgias. He had taken refuge in Italy, he said; but he abstained from supplying his exact address, though he offered to return and give evidence at the approaching trial at Rozan if he received a formal guarantee that his liberty would not be interfered with. In this second letter he still called Simon a loathsome Jew, and declared that he possessed overwhelming proof of his guilt, which proof, however, he would only divulge to the jury at the Assize Court. At the same time this did not prevent him from referring to his superiors, notably Father Crabot, in aggressive and outrageous terms fraught with all the bitter violence of an accomplice once willingly accepted but now cast off and sacrificed. How idiotic, said he, was their story of a forged school stamp! What a wretched falsehood, when the truth might well be told! They were fools and cowards, cowards especially, for had they not acted with the vilest cowardice in abandoning him, Gorgias, the faithful servant of God, after sacrificing both the heroic Father Philibin and the unhappy Brother Fulgence? Of the latter he only spoke in terms of indulgent contempt; Fulgence, said he, had been a sorry individual, unhinged, and full of vanity; and the others, after allowing him all freedom to compromise himself, had got rid of him by sending him to some distant spot under the pretext that he was ill. As for Father Philibin, Gorgias set him on a pinnacle, called him his friend, a hero of dutifulness, one who displayed passive obedience to his chiefs, who on their side employed him for the dirtiest work, and struck him down as soon as it was to their interest to close his mouth. And this hero, who was now suffering untold agony in a convent among the Apennines, was depicted by Gorgias as a martyr of the faith, even as he had been depicted in print, with a palm and a halo, by some of the ardent anti-Simonists.

From this point Gorgias proceeded to glorify himself with extraordinary vehemence, wild and splendid impudence. He became superb; he displayed such a mixture of frankness and falsehood, energy and duplicity, that, if the fates had been propitious, this base rascal might assuredly have become a great man. Even as his superiors were still pleased to admit, he remained a model cleric, full of admirable, exclusive, militant faith, one who assigned to the Church the royalty both of heaven and of earth, and who regarded himself as the Church's soldier, privileged to do everything in her defence. At the head of the Church was the Deity, then came his superiors and himself, and when he had given an account of his actions to his superiors and the Deity, the only thing left for the rest of the world was submission. Moreover, his superiors were of no account when he deemed them to be unworthy. In that case he remained alone in the presence of heaven. Thus, on days of confession, when God had absolved him, he regarded himself as the unique, the one pure man, who owed no account of his actions to anybody, and who was above all human laws. Was not this indeed the essential Catholic doctrine, according to which the ministers of the faith are rightly amenable to the divine authority alone? And was it not only a Father Crabot, full of social cowardice, who could trouble himself about imbecile human justice, and the stupid opinions of the multitude?

In this second letter, moreover, Brother Gorgias admitted, with a serene lack of shame, that he himself occasionally sinned. He then beat his breast, cried aloud that he was but a wolf and a hog, and humbly cast himself in the dust at the feet of God. Having thus made atonement, he became tranquil and continued to serve the Church in all holiness until the clay of creation cast him into sin again, whereupon fresh absolution became necessary. But in any case he was at least a loyal Catholic, he had the courage to confess, and the strength to endure penitence, whereas all those dignitaries of the Church, those Superiors of the Religious Orders, of whom he complained so bitterly, were liars and poltroons, who trembled before the consequences of their transgressions—who, like base hypocrites, concealed them or else cast them upon others in their terror of the judgment of men.

At the outset Brother Gorgias's passionate recriminations had seemed to be prompted merely by his anger at being so brutally abandoned after serving as a docile instrument; but at present veiled threats began to mingle with his reproaches. If he himself had always paid for his transgressions like a good Christian, there were others, he said, who had not done so. Yet some day assuredly they would be forced to make atonement, should they continue to try the patience of heaven, which would well know how to set up an avenger, a justiciary to proclaim the unconfessed, unpunished crimes. In saying this Gorgias was evidently alluding to Father Crabot and the mysterious story of the acquisition of the Countess de Quédeville's immense fortune—that splendid domain of Valmarie, where the Jesuit College had been subsequently established.

Several confused versions of that story had been current, and certain particulars were now recalled: The old but still beautiful Countess becoming extremely pious, and engaging Father Philibin, then a young man, as tutor to her grandson, Gaston, the last of the Quédevilles, who was barely nine years old. Next, Father Crabot arriving at the château and becoming the confessor, the friend, and some even said the lover, of the still beautiful Countess. Finally, the accident, the death of little Gaston, who had been drowned while walking out with his tutor, his death allowing his grandmother to bequeath the family estate and fortune to Father Crabot, through the medium of a clerical banker of Beaumont. And it was also remembered that among little Gaston's playmates there had been a gamekeeper's son, a lad named Georges Plumet, whom the Jesuits of Valmarie subsequently protected and assisted, and who was none other than the present Brother Gorgias.

The latter's violent language and threatening manner recalled all those half-forgotten incidents, and revived the old suspicion that some dark deed might link the gamekeeper's humble son to the powerful clerics who ruled the region. Would that not explain the protection which they had so long given him, the audacious manner in which they had shielded him, and at last even made his cause their own? Doubtless their first impulse had been to save the Church, but a little later they had done their utmost to make that terrible Ignorantine appear innocent; and if they had now sacrificed him, it must be because they deemed it impossible to defend him any longer. Perhaps, too, Brother Gorgias only wished to alarm them in order to wring from them as much money as possible. That he did alarm them was certain; one could detect that they were greatly disturbed by the letters and articles of that dreadful chatterer, who was ever ready to beat his breast and cry his sinfulness and that of others aloud. Moreover, in spite of the seeming abandonment in which he was left, one could divine that he was still protected, powerfully even if secretly; while his sudden intervals of silence, which lasted at times for weeks, plainly indicated that friendly messages and money had been sent to him.

His admissions and his threats quite upset the rank and file of the clerical faction. It was horrible! He profaned the temple, he exposed the secrets of the tabernacle to the unhealthy curiosity of unbelievers! Nevertheless, a good many devout folk remained attached to him, impressed by the uncompromising faith with which he bowed to God alone, and refused to recognise any of the so-called rights of human society. Besides, why should one not accept his version of the affair, his admission that he had really initialled the copy-slip, that it had been carried away by Zéphirin, and utilised by Simon for a diabolical purpose? This version was less ridiculous than that of his superiors: it even supplied an excuse for what Father Philibin had done, for one could picture the latter losing his head, and tearing off the stamped corner of the slip, in a moment of blind zeal for the safety of his holy mother, the Church.

To tell the truth, however, a far greater number of laymen, those who were faithful to Father Crabot, as well as nearly all the priests and other clerics clung stubbornly to the Jesuits' revised version of the incident—that of Simon forging the paraph, and using a false stamp. It was an absurd idea, but the readers of *Le Petit Beaumontais* became all the more impassioned over it, for the invention of a false stamp added yet another glaring improbability to the affair. Every morning the newspaper repeated imperturbably that material proofs existed of the making of that false stamp, and that the recondemnation of Simon by the Rozan Assize Court could no longer be a matter of doubt for anybody.

The rallying word had been passed round, and all 'right-minded' people made a show of believing that the Brothers' school would triumph as soon as the impious adversaries of the unfortunate Brother Gorgias should be confounded. The school greatly needed such a victory, for, discredited as it was by the semi-confessions and unpleasant discoveries of recent times, it had just lost two more of its pupils. Only the final overthrow of Simon and his return to the galleys could restore its lustre. Until then it was fit that Brother Fulgence's successor should remain patiently in the background, while Father Théodose, the Superior of the Capuchins,—who also triumphed, even when others were being ruined,—skilfully exploited the situation by urging his devotees to make little periodical offerings, such for instance as two francs a month, to St. Antony of Padua, in order that the saint might exert his influence to keep the good Brothers' school at Maillebois.

However, the most serious incident of the turmoil in the town was supplied by Abbé Quandieu, who had long been regarded as a prudent Simonist. At that time it had been said that Monseigneur Bergerot, the Bishop, was behind him, even as Father Crabot was behind the Capuchins and the Brothers of the Christian Doctrine. As usual, indeed, the Seculars and the Regulars confronted each other, the priests resenting the efforts which were made by the monks to divert all worship and revenue to their own profit. And in this instance, as in fact in all others, the better cause was that of the priests, whose conception of the religion of Christ was more equitable and human than that of the monks. Nevertheless, Monseigneur Bergerot had been defeated, and by his advice Abbé Quandieu had submitted and had done penance by attending an idolatrous ceremony at the Capuchin Chapel.

But all the disastrous disclosures and occurrences of recent times—first Father Philibin shown guilty of perjury and forgery, then Brother Fulgence spirited away after compromising himself, then, too, Brother Gorgias absconding and almost confessing his guilt—had stirred the parish priest of Maillebois to rebellion, and revived his former belief in Simon's innocence. Nevertheless he would probably have remained silent, in a spirit of discipline, if Abbé Cognasse, the priest of Jonville, had not gone out of his way to allude to him in a sermon, saying that an apostate priest, a hireling of the Jews, a traitor to his God and his country, was unhappily at the head of a neighbouring parish. On hearing this, Abbé Quandieu's Christian ardour asserted itself; he could no longer control the grief he felt at seeing 'the dealers of the Temple,' as he called them, betraying the Saviour who was all truth and justice. Thus, in his sermon on the following Sunday, he spoke of certain baleful men who were slaying the Church by their abominable complicity with the perpetrators of the vilest crimes. One may picture the scandal, the agitation, that ensued in the clerical world, particularly as it was asserted that Monseigneur Bergerot was again behind Abbé Quandieu, and was determined this time that fanatical and malignant sectarians should not be allowed to compromise religion any further.

At last, while passion was thus running riot, the new trial began before the Rozan Assize Court. It had been possible to bring Simon back to France, though he was still ailing, imperfectly cured as yet of the exhausting fevers which had delayed his return for nearly a year. During the voyage it had been feared that he would not be put ashore alive. Moreover, for fear of disorder, violence, and outrage, it had been necessary to practise dissimulation with respect to the spot where he would land, and bring him to Rozan at night time by roundabout ways which none suspected. At present he was in prison near the Palace of Justice, having only a street to cross in order to appear before his judges. And pending that event he was closely watched and guarded, defended also, like the important and disquieting personage he had become, one with whose fate that of the whole nation was bound up.

The first person privileged to see him was Rachel his wife, whom that reunion, after so many frightful years, cast into wild emotion. Ah! what an embrace they exchanged! And how great was the grief she displayed after that visit, so thin, so weak had she found him, so aged, too, with his white hair! And he had showed himself so strange, ignorant as he still was of the facts, for the brief communication by which the Court of Cassation had informed him of the approaching revision of his case had given no particulars. It had not surprised him to hear of the revision, he had always felt that it would some day take place; and this conviction, in spite of all his tortures, had lent him the strength to live in order that he might once more see his children and give them back a spotless name. But how dark was the anguish in which he had remained plunged, his mind ever dwelling on the frightful enigma of his condemnation, which he could not unravel! His brother David and Advocate Delbos, who hastened to the prison, ended by acquainting him with the whole monstrous affair, the terrible war which had been waged for years respecting his case, between those perpetual foes, the men of authoritarian views who defended the rotten edifice of the past, and the men of free thought who went towards the future. Then only did Simon understand the truth and come to regard his personal sufferings as mere incidents, whose only importance arose from the fact that they had led to a splendid uprising in the name of justice, which would benefit all mankind. Moreover, he did not willingly speak of his torments; he had suffered less from his companions, the thieves and murderers around him, than from his keepers, those ferocious brutes who were left free to act as they pleased, and who, like disciples of the Marquis de Sade, took a voluptuous delight in torturing and killing with impunity. Had it not been for the strength of resistance which Simon owed to racial heredity, and his cold logical temperament, he would twenty times have provoked his custodians to shoot him dead. And at present he talked of all those things in a quiet way, and evinced a naïve astonishment on being told of the extraordinary complications of the drama of which he was the victim.

Having secured a citation as a witness, Marc obtained leave of absence, and, a few days before the trial began, he took up his abode at Rozan, where he found David and Delbos already in the thick of the supreme battle. He was surprised by the nervousness and anxious thoughtfulness of David, who was usually so brave and calm. And it seemed to him that Delbos, as a rule so gaily valiant, was likewise uneasy. As a matter of fact it was for the latter a very big affair, in which he risked both his position as an advocate and his increasing popularity as a Socialist leader. If he should win the case he would doubtless end by beating Lemarrois at Beaumont; but unfortunately all sorts of disquieting symptoms were becoming manifest. Indeed Marc himself, after reaching Rozan full of hope, soon began to feel alarmed amid his new surroundings.

Elsewhere, even at Maillebois, the acquittal of Simon appeared certain to everybody possessed of any sense. Father Crabot's clients, in their private converse, did not conceal the fact that they felt their cause to be greatly endangered. The best news also came from Paris, where the Ministers regarded a just *dénouement* as certain, lulled into confidence as they were by their agents' reports respecting the Court and the jury. But the atmosphere was very different at Rozan, where an odour of falsehood and treachery pervaded the streets, and found its way into the depths of men's souls. This town, once the capital of a province, and now greatly fallen from its former importance, had retained all its monarchical and religious faith, all the antiquated fanaticism of a past age, which elsewhere had disappeared. [2] Thus it supplied an excellent battle-ground for the Congregations, which absolutely needed a decisive victory if they were to retain their teaching privileges and control the future. And never had Marc more fully realised how deeply Rome was interested in winning that battle; never had he more plainly detected that behind the slightest incidents of that interminable and monstrous affair there was papal Rome, clinging stubbornly to its dream of universal domination—Rome which, at every step over the paving-stones of Rozan, he found at work there, whispering, striving, and conquering.

> [2] If proof were wanted to show that by Rozan M. Zola means Rennes, the fanatical ex-capital of Brittany, it would be found in the passage given above.—*Trans.*

Delbos and David advised him to observe extreme prudence. They themselves were guarded by detectives for fear of some ambush; and he, on the very morrow of his arrival, found shadowy forms hovering around him. Was he not Simon's successor, the secular schoolmaster, the enemy of which the Church must rid itself if it desired to triumph? And the stealthy hatred by which Marc felt himself to be encompassed, the menace of an evil blow in some dark corner, sufficed to show him that the battle had sunk to the very lowest level, and that his adversaries were indeed those men of blind, bigoted violence, who through the ages had tortured, burnt, and murdered their fellow-beings in their mad dream of staying the march of mankind!

That much established, Marc understood the terror weighing on the town, the dismal aspect of its houses, whose shutters remained closed, as if an epidemic were raging. As a rule, there is little animation in Rozan during the summer, and at that moment the town seemed emptier than ever.

Pedestrians hastened their steps, glancing anxiously around them as they went their way in the broad sunshine; shopkeepers stood at their windows, inspecting the streets as if they feared some massacre. The selection of the jury particularly upset those trembling folk; there was much melancholy jogging of heads when the names of the chosen jurors were made public. It was evidently considered a disaster to have one among one's relatives.

Churchgoers abounded among the petty *rentiers*, manufacturers, and tradespeople of that clerical centre, where lack of religion was regarded as a shameful blot, and proved extremely prejudicial to one's pecuniary interests. Frantic was the pressure exercised by mothers and wives, led by all the priests, abbés, and monks of the six parish churches and the thirty convents, whose bells were always ringing. At Beaumont, in former times, the Church had been obliged to work with some discretion, for it had found itself in the presence of both an old Voltairean *bourgeoisie* and of revolutionary *faubourgs*. But there was no need for it to beat about the bush in that sleepy city of Rozan, whose traditions were entirely pious. The workmen's wives went to Mass, the women of the middle class formed all sorts of religious associations; and thus a holy crusade began; none refused to help in defeating Simon. A week before the trial the whole town had become a battlefield; there was not a house that did not witness some combat waged for the good cause. The wretched jurors shut themselves up, no longer daring to go out, for strangers accosted them in the streets, terrified them with evil glances or passing words, in which there lurked a threat to punish them in their pockets or their persons if they did not behave as good Catholics, and re-condemn the dirty Jew.

Marc was rendered yet more anxious by some information he received respecting Counsellor Guybaraud, who was to preside over the Assize Court, and Procureur Pacart, who was to conduct the prosecution. The first had been a pupil of the Valmarie Jesuits, to whom he owed his rapid promotion, and had married a very wealthy and very pious hunchbacked girl, whom he had received from their hands. The latter, an ex-demagogue, had been vaguely compromised in some gambling affair, and, becoming a frantic anti-semite, had rallied to the Church, from which he expected a post in Paris. Marc felt particularly distrustful of Pacart on observing how insidiously the anti-Simonists affected anxiety respecting his attitude, as if indeed they feared some revival of his revolutionary past. While they never ceased praising the lofty conscientiousness of Guybaraud, they spoke of Pacart with all sorts of reservations, in order, no doubt, to enable him to play the heroic part of an honest man, overcome by the force of truth, on the day when he would have to ask the jury for Simon's head. The very circumstance that the clericals went about Rozan dolefully repeating that

Pacart was not on their side made Marc distrustful, for information from a good source had acquainted him with the undoubted venality of this man, who was ready for the vilest bargaining in his eager desire to regain a semblance of honour in some high position.

However, the desperate and deadly battle became at Rozan a subterranean one. The affair was not lightly prosecuted in drawing-rooms among the smiles of ladies, as at Beaumont. Nor was there any question of a liberal prelate like Monseigneur Bergerot resisting the Congregations from a dread lest the Church should be submerged and swept away by the rising tide of base superstition. This time the contest was carried on in the darkness in which great social crimes take their course; all that appeared on the surface was some turbid ebullition, a kind of terror sweeping through the streets as through a city stricken with a pestilence. And Marc's anguish arose particularly from that circumstance. Instead of again witnessing the resounding clash of Simonists and anti-Simonists, as at Beaumont, he was confronted by the stealthy preparations for a dark crime, for which a Guybaraud and a Pacart were doubtless the necessary chosen instruments.

Every evening David and Delbos repaired to the large room which Marc had rented in a lonely street, and ardent friends of all classes surrounded them. These formed the little sacred phalanx; each visitor brought some news, contributed suggestions and courage. They were determined that they would not despair. Indeed, after an evening spent together they felt inspirited, ready for fresh encounters. And they were aware that their enemies met in a neighbouring street, at the house of a brother-in-law of Judge Gragnon, who, having been summoned as a witness by the defence, was staying there, receiving all the militant anti-Simonists of the town—a procession of frocks and gowns that slipped into the house as soon as night had fallen. Father Crabot had slept there twice, it was said, and had then returned to Valmarie, where with a great display of humility he had cloistered himself in penitence.

Suspicious characters prowled about that sparsely populated district; the streets were not safe; and, accordingly, when David and Delbos quitted Marc at night, their friends accompanied them home in a band. One night a shot was fired; but the detectives, though always on the watch, could find nobody to arrest. But the favourite weapon of the priests is venomous slander, moral murder, perpetrated in a cowardly fashion in the dark. And Delbos became the chosen victim. On the very day when the trial was to begin, the number of *Le Petit Beaumontais* which reached Rozan contained an abominable disclosure, full of mendacity, a shamefully travestied story, half a century old, about the advocate's father. The elder Delbos, though of peasant stock, had become a goldsmith, in a small way, in the neighbourhood of the Bishop's residence at Beaumont; and the newspaper charged him with having made away with certain sacred vessels which had been entrusted to him for repair. The truth was that the goldsmith, robbed by a woman whom he was unwilling to denounce, had found himself obliged to pay the value of the stolen goods. There had been no prosecution; the affair had remained obscure; but one had to read that filthy print to realise to what depths of malevolence and ignominy certain men could descend. That painful, forgotten, buried misfortune of the father's was cast in the face of the son with an abundance of spurious particulars, vile imaginings, set forth in language which was all outrage and mire. And the desecrator of the grave, the murderously-minded libeller who wrote those things, had plainly obtained the documents he published from the very hands of Father Crabot, to whom they had been communicated, no doubt, by some priestly archivist. It was hoped that this unexpected bludgeon-blow would strike Delbos full in the heart, assassinate him morally, discredit him as an advocate, annihilate him to such a point that he would have neither the strength to speak nor the authority to gain a hearing in the defence of Simon.

However, the trial began one Monday, a hot day in July. Apart from Gragnon, whom it was intended to confront with Jacquin, the foreman of the first jury, several witnesses had been cited for the defence. Mignot, Mlle. Rouzaire, Daix, Mauraisin, Salvan, Sébastien and Victor Milhomme, Polydor Souquet, the younger Bongards, Doloirs, and Savins were all on the list. Fathers Crabot and Philibin, Brothers Fulgence and Gorgias had also been cited, though it was known that the last three would not appear. On the other side the Procureur de la République had contented himself with recalling the witnesses for the prosecution who had given evidence at the first trial. And the streets of Rozan had at last become animated with witnesses, journalists, and inquisitive folk, arriving in fresh batches by each succeeding train. Already at six o'clock in the morning a crowd assembled near the Palace of Justice eager to catch a glimpse of Simon. But a considerable military force had been set on foot, the street was cleared, and Simon crossed it between two rows of soldiers, set so closely together that none of the onlookers could distinguish his features. It was then eight o'clock. That early hour had been chosen in order to avoid the oppressive heat of the afterpart of the day when one would have stifled in the court-room.

The scene was very different from that presented by the brand new assize-hall of Beaumont, where a profusion of gilding had glittered in the crude light that streamed in by the lofty windows. At Rozan the assizes were held in an ancient feudal castle; the hall was small and low, panelled with old oak, and scarcely lighted by the windows of a few deep bays. One might have thought the place to be one of those dark chapels where the Inquisition pronounced sentence. Only a few ladies could possibly be admitted, and all of them, moreover, wore sombre garb. Most of the seats were occupied by the witnesses, and even the little standing-room usually allowed to the public had to be curtailed. The audience, packed since seven o'clock in that stern and mournful room, preserved a relative silence, through which swept a stealthy quiver. If the eyes of the onlookers remained ardent their gestures were restrained; they had come there for a subterranean execution, a work of suppression which had to be accomplished far from the light, with the least noise possible.

As soon as Marc was seated beside David, who went in with the witnesses, he experienced a feeling of anguish, a stifling sensation, as if the walls were about to crumble and bury them. He had seen all eyes turn in their direction. David, particularly, aroused great curiosity. Then Marc felt moved, for Delbos had just come in, looking pale but resolute amid the evil glances of most of the spectators, who were eager to ascertain if he had been upset by the infamous article which had appeared that morning. However, the advocate, as if arrayed in an armour of valour and contempt, remained for some time standing there, displaying only smiling strength and indifference.

Marc then interested himself in the jurors, scrutinising them as they entered, one by one, anxious as he was to ascertain to what kind of men the great task of reparation was confided. And he perceived the insignificant faces of various petty tradespeople, petty *bourgeois,* with a chemist, a veterinary surgeon, and two retired captains. On all those faces one found an expression of mournful disquietude, the signs of a desire to hide internal perturbation. The worries which had assailed those men since their names had become known had pursued them to that hall. Several had the wan countenances of devotees, of shaven, canting beadles, while others, red and corpulent, looked as if they had doubled their usual ration of brandy that morning in order to instil a little courage into their paunches. Behind them one could divine the entirety of that old priestly and military city with its convents and its barracks; and one shuddered to think that those men, whose minds and consciences had been deformed, stifled, by their surroundings, should be entrusted with such a work of justice.

But a buzzing spread through the hall, and all at once Marc experienced the most poignant thrill of emotion he had ever known. He had not seen Simon since his return, and now he suddenly perceived him, standing behind Delbos. And terrible was the apparition of that bent and emaciated little man, with ravaged features and bald cranium, on which only a few scanty white locks remained. What! that wreck, that puny remnant of a man was his old comrade, whom he had known so vivacious and refined! If Simon had never possessed any great physical gifts, if his voice had been weak, his gestures inelegant, at least a brazier of youth and faith had glowed within him. And the galleys had only given back that poor, broken, crushed being, a mere shred of humanity, in whom nought of the past subsisted save two flaming eyes, which alone proclaimed the invincible will and courage he preserved. One recognised him only by those eyes; and they, too, explained how he had been able for so many years to resist suffering, for their expression told of the world of fancy, of pure ideality, in which he had always lived. Every glance was turned upon him, but he did not seem conscious of it, such was the power he possessed of isolating himself. He gazed at the assembly in an absent-minded way until at last a smile of infinite tenderness came over his face as he perceived his brother David. Marc, who sat beside the latter, then felt him tremble in every limb.

It was a quarter past eight o'clock when the usher's call rang out, and the Court entered. The assembly arose and then sat down again. Marc, who remembered the violence of the spectators at Beaumont, who from growls had passed to vociferations, was astonished by the heavy quietude preserved by the present onlookers, though he divined that they were swayed by the same passions, and remained mutely eager for slaughter, as if they were lying in ambush in some sombre nook. The sight of the prisoner had scarcely wrung a low murmur from them; and now while the judges took their seats, they relapsed into their attitude of dark expectancy. Again, compared with the rough and jovial Gragnon, the new presiding judge, Guybaraud, surprised one by his perfect courtesy, his unctuous gestures, his insinuating speech. He was a little man, whose manner was all smiles and gentleness, but an odour of the sacristies seemed to emanate from his person, and his grey eyes were as cold and as cutting as steel. Nor was the difference less remarkable between the former Procureur de la République, the brilliant Raoul de La Bissonnière, and Pacart, the present one, who was very long, slender, and lean, with a yellow, baked face, as if he were consumed by a desire to efface his equivocal past and make a rapid fortune.

After the first formalities, when the jury had been empanelled, an usher called the names of the witnesses, who, one by one, withdrew. Marc, like the others, had to leave the hall. Then, in a leisurely way, President Guybaraud began to interrogate Simon, putting his questions in a tone of voice that suggested the coldness of a blade, handled with deadly skill and precision. That interminable examination, which lingered over the slightest incidents of the old affair, and insisted on the charge which the inquiry of the Court of Cassation had destroyed, proved quite a surprise. Some clearing of the ground, an examination on the questions set by the supreme jurisdiction, was all that had been expected; but it at once became evident that the Assize Court of Rozan did not intend to take any account of the facts established by that jurisdiction, and that the presiding judge meant to avail himself of his discretionary powers to deal with the entire case from the very beginning. Soon, indeed, by the questions which he asked, one understood that nothing of the old indictment had been relinquished. It was again alleged that Simon had returned from Beaumont by rail, that he had reached Maillebois at twenty minutes to eleven o'clock, and that soon afterwards he had committed the crime. At this point, however, the new version of the Jesuits—necessitated by the discovery at Father Philibin's—was interpolated, and the prisoner was accused of having procured a copy-slip, of having caused a false stamp to be made, and of having forged on the slip the initials of Brother Gorgias. Thus that childish story, which Gorgias himself had deemed so idiotic that he had admitted the authenticity of the slip and the paraph, was retained. While nothing was abandoned of the original charges, a gross invention was brought forward in support of them; and everything was again based on the famous report of the experts, Masters Badoche and Trabut, who clung to their original statements in spite of Brother Gorgias's formal admissions. And the Procureur de la République, as if to leave no doubt of his own views, intervened in order to extract precise statements from the prisoner with respect to his denials on the question of the false stamp.

Simon's demeanour during that long examination was regarded as pitiful. Many of his partisans had dreamt of him as a justiciar, armed with the thunderbolts of heaven, and rising like an avenger from the grave into which he had been thrust by iniquitous hands. And as he answered politely in a voice which still quivered feverishly, and with none of the outbursts that had been anticipated, the disappointment was extreme. His enemies once more began to say that he virtually confessed his crime, the ignominy of which they found stamped upon his unprepossessing countenance. Only at one moment did he become excited, display any passionate fervour. This was when the judge spoke to him of the false stamp of which he heard for the first time. It should be added that no proof was supplied respecting that stamp; the prosecution contented itself with relating that an unknown workman had confided to a woman that he had secretly done a curious job for the schoolmaster of Maillebois. Confronted, however, by the sudden violence of Simon, the judge did not insist on the point, particularly as Delbos had risen, prepared to raise an 'incident.' And the public prosecutor merely added that, though they had failed to find the unknown workman, he reserved to himself the right of insisting on the serious probability of the alleged occurrence.

In the evening, when David related what had occurred at that first sitting, Marc, who divined some fresh iniquity, felt a pang at the heart. Assuredly the greatest crime of all was now in preparation. He was not astonished by the calm and unobtrusive bearing of Simon, who was confident in the strength of his innocence, and incapable of an outward show of emotion. [3] But he perfectly understood the bad effect which had been produced; while, from the aggressive coldness of the presiding judge, and the importance the latter gave to the most trivial matters, already elucidated, he derived a disastrous impression, a quasi-certainty that a fresh conviction was impending. On hearing him, David, from whom he thought it wrong to hide his anxiety, could only with difficulty restrain his tears, for he also had quitted the Palace of Justice in despair, full of a dreadful presentiment.

> [3] This was a marked characteristic of the unfortunate Captain Dreyfus, whose demeanour at the trial at Rennes produced such an unfavourable impression on sundry foolish English 'special correspondents,' that they veered round and began to regard the prisoner as guilty, quite irrespective of the evidence. As one who has witnessed many criminal trials, who has been a juror and the foreman of a jury, I feel that everything that has been written to my knowledge in English literature respecting the 'proper' demeanour of an innocent man is nonsense and nothing else.—*Trans.*.

However, the following days, which were entirely devoted to the hearing of evidence, brought back some courage and illusion. The former witnesses for the prosecution were first examined, and one again beheld a procession of railway employés and *octroi* officials, who contradicted one another on the question whether Simon, on the night of the crime, had returned to Maillebois by train or on foot. Marc, who wished to follow the case, had asked Delbos to have him called as soon as possible, and this being done he gave evidence respecting the discovery of poor little Zéphirin's body. He was then able to seat himself once more beside David, who still occupied a corner of the small space allotted to the witnesses. And thus Marc was present at the first 'incident' raised by the counsel for the defence, who had retained all his bravery and self-possession in spite of the cruel blow which had lately struck him in the heart.

He rose to demand the attendance of Father Philibin and Brothers Fulgence and Gorgias, who, said he, had been duly cited. But the presiding judge briefly explained that the citations had reached neither Father Philibin nor Brother Gorgias, both of whom, no doubt, were abroad, though their exact whereabouts was not known. As for Brother Fulgence, he was seriously ill, and had sent a medical certificate to that effect. Delbos insisted, however, with respect to Brother Fulgence, and ended by obtaining a promise that he should be visited by a sworn medical man. Then, also, the advocate was unwilling to content himself with a letter in which Father Crabot, while urging his occupations, his confessional duties, as an excuse for absence, declared that he knew nothing whatever of the affair; and, in spite of the acrimonious intervention of the Procureur de la République, Delbos again carried his point—that the Court should insist on the attendance of the Rector of Valmarie. However, this first collision fomented anger, and from that moment conflicts continually arose between the judge and the advocate.

The day's sitting ended amidst an outburst of emotion, occasioned by the unexpected character of the evidence given by assistant-teacher Mignot. Mademoiselle Rouzaire, as bitter and as positive as ever, had just reaffirmed that, at about twenty minutes to eleven o'clock, she had heard the footsteps and the voice of Simon coming in and speaking with Zéphirin—which evidence had weighed so heavily on the prisoner at the previous trial—when Mignot, following her at the bar, retracted the whole of his former statements in a tone of wondrous frankness and emotion. He had heard nothing; he was now convinced of Simon's innocence, and adduced the weightiest reasons. Mademoiselle Rouzaire was then recalled, and there came a dramatic confrontation, in which the schoolmistress ended by losing ground, becoming embarrassed in her estimate of the hour, and finding nothing to answer when Mignot pointed out that it was impossible to hear from her room anything that took place in little Zéphirin's. Marc was recalled to confirm Mignot's demonstration, and at the bar he found himself for a moment beside Inspector Mauraisin, who, being asked for his opinion respecting the prisoner and the witnesses, endeavoured to get out of his difficulty by indulging in extravagant praise of Mademoiselle Rouzaire's merits, while saying nothing particular against Mignot or Marc, or even Simon, at a loss as he was to tell what turn the case might take.

The next two sittings of the Court proved even better for the defence. The question of hearing a part of the evidence *in camera*, which had impassioned people at the first trial, was not even put, for the presiding judge did not dare to raise it. It was in public that he interrogated Simon's former pupils, boys at the time of the crime but now grown men, for the most part married. Fernand Bongard, Auguste and Charles Doloir, Achille and Philippe Savin came in succession to relate the little they remembered, and their statements were favourable to the prisoner rather than the reverse. Thus ended the abominable legend built up by the help of the former proceedings *in camera*, the legend of horrible charges with which, it had been said, one could not possibly soil the ears of an audience composed partially of women.

However, the sensational evidence of the sitting was that given by Sébastien and Victor Milhomme. In accents of emotion Sébastien, now two and twenty years of age, explained the falsehood of his childhood, the alarm of his mother, the suppression of the truth, which he and she had expiated after prolonged torture. And he stated the facts such as they really were, how he had seen a copy-slip in the hands of his cousin Victor, how that slip had disappeared, how it had been found again, and given up when his mother, grief-stricken beside his bed of sickness, had deemed herself punished for her bad action. As for Victor, when his turn came to testify, in order to please his mother, who did not wish to compromise the stationery business any further, he feigned total forgetfulness, the obtuseness of a big fellow who had no memory. No doubt he must have brought the copy-slip from the Brothers' school, as it had been found, but he knew nothing, he could say nothing further.

Finally, another of the Brothers' former pupils, Polydor Souquet, now a servant in a Beaumont convent, appeared at the bar, and was questioned very pressingly by Delbos respecting the manner in which Brother Gorgias had escorted him home on the night of the crime, the incidents which had occurred on the road, the words that had been exchanged, and the hour. But all that Delbos could extract from Polydor were some evasive answers, and malicious glances promptly tempered by an affectation of stupidity. How could one remember after so many years? the witness asked. The excuse was too convenient, and the Procureur de la République began to show signs of anxious impatience, while the onlookers, though they failed to understand why the advocate insisted so much with an apparently insignificant witness, felt as it were a quiver of the truth passing through the atmosphere—the truth suspected, but once more taking flight.

People were stirred again at the next sitting of the Court, though it began with the interminable demonstrations of the experts, Masters Badoche and Trabut, who, disregarding even the admissions of Brother Gorgias himself, obstinately refused to recognise his initials, an F and a G, in the incriminated paraph, in which they alone recognised those of Simon, an E and an S interlaced, but, it was true, illegible. For more than three hours these men piled argument upon argument, demonstration on demonstration, calmly persevering in their lunacy. And the marvel was that the presiding judge allowed them to go on, and listened to them with manifest complacency, while the Procureur made a show of taking notes, and asked the experts for precise information on certain points, as if the prosecution still adopted their system. In presence of this *mise-en-scène*, even reasonable people in the hall began to hesitate. And, after all, why not? For in matters of handwriting one could never tell.

But at the close of the sitting an incident, which did not last ten minutes, upset everybody. Clad in black from head to foot, ex-investigating Magistrate Daix, who had been cited by the defence, appeared at the bar. He was scarcely fifty-six years old, but he looked seventy; thin and bent, his hair quite white, his face so emaciated that little of it, save the slender, blade-like nose, seemed to remain. He had lately lost his wife, and people talked of the torturing life which that ugly, coquettish, ambitious woman had led him in her despair that nothing ever raised them from their narrow circumstances, not even the condemnation of that Jew Simon, on which she had insisted and from which she had hoped to derive so much. And now that his wife was no longer beside him, Daix, timid and anxious, painstaking in his profession, an honest man at heart, had come there to relieve his conscience, distracted as he was by the deeds which had been wrung from his weakness, his craving to have peace at home. He did not positively speak of all those things, he did not even admit that after his investigations he had felt that the only possible decision was an order to stay further proceedings. But he allowed Delbos to question him, and when his present opinion was asked, he replied plainly that the inquiry of the Court of Cassation had destroyed his work, the original indictment, and that for his own part he now regarded Simon as innocent. Then he withdrew amidst the silent stupefaction of the onlookers. The apparition of that man in mourning garb, the admissions made by him in slow and sorrowful accents, had stirred every heart.

That evening, in Marc's large room, where Simon's friends met after every sitting of the Court in order to discuss matters, Delbos and David expressed keen satisfaction, a conviction that success was almost certain now, so great, apparently, was the impression which Daix's evidence had produced on the jury. Nevertheless, Marc remained anxious. He told the others of certain rumours which were circulating concerning the stealthy doings of ex-President Gragnon, who had been carrying on a subterranean campaign ever since his arrival at Rozan. Marc was aware that, even as the friends of the defence met in his own room, in like way mysterious meetings took place every night at Gragnon's in an adjoining street. And there the partisans of the prosecution certainly decided on the line they would pursue on the morrow, invented the answers which it would be best to give, planned the incidents which they felt ought to be raised, in particular preparing the evidence in accordance with the result of the day's sitting. For instance, whenever that sitting was regarded as unfavourable to the prosecution, one might be sure that there would be some surprise detrimental to the prisoner, at the outset of the sitting on the morrow. Moreover, Father Crabot had been again seen slipping into Gragnon's house. Several people also declared that they had seen young Polydor Souquet leaving it. And others alleged that at a very late hour they had met in the street a lady and a gentleman who looked extremely like Mademoiselle Rouzaire and Inspector Mauraisin. But the worst was some mysterious work, which centred round those jurors who were notoriously on the side of the Church, and of which Marc obtained an inkling, though his informant could not give him full particulars. Gragnon did not commit such a blunder as to ask those men to call at his house, nor did he, indeed, address himself to them personally; but he made others call on them, and show them, so it was said, an irrefutable proof of Simon's guilt, a terrible document, which the most serious reasons prevented him from making public, though he was resolved to employ it, all the same, should the defence drive him to extremities. And this information made Marc feel anxious, for he scented some fresh abomination in it. Thus, on the evening of the day when Daix had dealt the prosecution such a severe blow, he predicted to his friends some deed of retaliation on the enemy's part, some sample of the thunder which Gragnon, according to his own account, had in his pocket.

The following sitting of the Court was, indeed, one of the gravest and most exciting. Jacquin, the foreman of the first jury, in his turn came forward to relieve his conscience. In simple language he related how President Gragnon, on being summoned by the jurors, who had wished to consult him respecting the penalty attaching to their verdict, had entered their room carrying a letter, and looking very much disturbed. And he had shown them that letter, which bore Simon's signature, followed by a postscriptum and a paraph, which last was identical with the one on the copy-slip tendered as evidence. Several jurymen, who had hesitated previously, then declared themselves convinced of the prisoner's guilt. He, Jacquin, had retained no further doubts; and for the peace of his conscience he had been well pleased at thus acquiring certainty. At that time he had not known that such a communication was illegal. It was only later that he had discovered such to be the case, and had experienced great distress of mind until, at last, the postscriptum and the paraph being recognised as forgeries, he had resolved, like a good Christian, to make amends for his involuntary error. A shudder of awe sped through those who heard him, when in his quiet way he added a last detail: He had heard the very voice of Jesus telling him to speak out, one evening when, tortured by remorse, he was kneeling in a dim chapel of St. Maxence.

Then Gragnon was summoned to the bar, and at first tried the effect of the rough frankness which he had so often assumed in his browbeating judicial days. He was still fat, though his fears had made him pale; and, striving to hide his prolonged anguish beneath the impudence of a *bon vivant*, he pretended that he no longer remembered petty details. And well—yes, he believed he had gone into the jurors' room carrying the letter which he had just received. He had been upset by it, and had shown it to the others in a moment of emotion, scarcely realising the nature of his action, and being only desirous of establishing the truth. He had never regretted that communication, so fully was he convinced of the authenticity of the postscript and the paraph. In his opinion the assertion that they were forgeries remained to be proved. Then, as he formally charged Jacquin with having read the letter aloud to the other jurors, and of having commented on it, the ex-foreman was recalled, and a sharp dispute ensued. At last Gragnon convicted the architect of some error or forgetfulness respecting the perusal of the letter; and thereupon he triumphed while the spectators began to hiss the honest witness, who from that moment was suspected of having sold himself to the Jews.

In vain did Delbos repeatedly intervene, striving to exasperate Gragnon and unmask him, by forcing him to an explosion, the production of the famous document which it was said would clench everything. The ex-judge, who retained all his self-possession, and who was satisfied with having escaped immediate danger by casting a doubt on his adversary's veracity, relapsed into evasive answers. It was noticed, however, that one of the jurors caused a question to be put to him—a question which nobody understood, but which was whether he did not possess some knowledge of another document bearing on the authenticity of the copy-slip. Gragnon answered enigmatically, that he abided by his previous declarations, and was unwilling to enter into other matters, however certain they might be. And thus that sitting of the Court, which, at the outset, had seemed likely to ruin the prosecution, ended to its advantage. In Marc's room in the evening, Simon's friends again began to despair.

The examination of the witnesses dragged on during a few more sittings. The doctor appointed to visit Brother Fulgence had returned with a report that the Brother's condition was very serious, and that it was impossible to bring him to Rozan. In like manner Father Crabot avoided the embarrassment of attendance by feigning a sudden accident—a severe sprain. In vain did Delbos make an application for his evidence to be taken by commission. President Guybaraud, who at the outset had shown himself so phlegmatic, now sabred everybody and everything in his eagerness to bring the case to an end. He treated Simon harshly, as if, indeed, he were already a condemned man; being emboldened to this course by the singular calmness of the prisoner, who still listened to the witnesses with curiosity and stupefaction, as if the extraordinary adventures of somebody else were being recounted to him. Only on two or three occasions did some extremely mendacious testimony prompt him to a little rebellion; for the most part he contented himself with smiling and shrugging his shoulders.

At last Pacart, the Procureur de la République, addressed the Court. Tall and thin, he was addicted to long, nervous gestures, and affected an unadorned, mathematically precise kind of eloquence. In presence of the plainly-worded judgment of the Court of Cassation, his task was not easy. But his tactics were very simple, he took no account of that judgment, he did not once allude to the long inquiry which had ended in a decision to send the affair for trial by another Assize Court. He quietly reverted to the old indictment, based himself on the report of the experts, and accepted the revised account of the copy-slip, holding that the school-stamp as well as the initialling had been forged. He even spoke of that stamp in a positive way, as if he held a proof that it had been forged but could not produce it. As for Brother Gorgias, he regarded him simply as an unfortunate man, perhaps mentally unhinged, assuredly in need, and of a passionate nature—one who, after proving an undisciplined and compromising son of the Church, had quitted it and sold himself to the Jews. And Pacart concluded by asking the jurors to put an end to this affair, which was so disastrous for the peace of the country, by saying once more on which side the culprit really was, whether among the Anarchists and the Cosmopolites—who sought to destroy all belief in God and country—or among the men upholding faith, respect, and tradition, to whom, for ages past, France had owed her grandeur.

Then Delbos spoke during two sittings. Eager and nervous, endowed with passionate eloquence, he also dealt with the affair from the very beginning. But he did so in order to destroy the allegations in the old indictment, with the help of the arguments supplied by the Court of Cassation's inquiry. Not one of those allegations was worth anything. It was proved that Simon had returned home on foot on the night of the crime; that he had reached Maillebois at twenty minutes to twelve o'clock, an hour after the crime had been committed. Again, there was proof that the copy-slip had been stamped at the Brothers' school and initialled by Brother Gorgias, whose admissions on the subject were not even necessary, for counter experts, in a memorable report addressed to the Court of Cassation, had destroyed the extraordinary farrago of Masters Badoche and Trabut. Then Delbos turned to the new story of the forged stamp. No proof of this had been supplied. Nevertheless, he insisted on the subject; for he divined that some supreme abomination lurked beneath all that stealthy manœuvring compounded of mere allegation and reticence. A sick workman, it was said, had told a woman a vague story about a stamp which he had made for the Maillebois schoolmaster. Where was that woman? Who was she? What was her calling? As nobody would or could reply, he (Delbos) had a right to conclude that this story was one of those absurd lies such as *Le Petit Beaumontais* was in the habit of retailing. However, if he was able to picture the whole crime as it must have taken place—Brother Gorgias returning after he had escorted Polydor home, pausing before Zéphirin's open window, finally entering the room, and at last succumbing to his ungovernable passions—he admitted that there was a gap in his narrative. Where had Gorgias found the copy-slip? For the rascal was right when he jeeringly inquired if schoolmasters usually walked about in the evening with copy-slips in their pockets. Undoubtedly the number of *Le Petit Beaumontais* had been in the pocket of his own cassock, whence he had taken it in order to gag his victim. And the slip must have been there also. But how had that happened? Delbos suspected the truth, and if he had questioned Polydor Souquet so pressingly it was in order to extract it from him. He had failed in that endeavour, the witness having met him with an assumption of hypocritical stupidity. But, after all, what did that obscure point matter? Was not Gorgias's guilt absolutely manifest? His alleged alibi was based solely on a series of false statements. Everything proved his guilt—his flight, his semi-confessions, the criminal efforts made to save him, and the dispersal of his accomplices—Father Philibin hiding himself in some Italian convent; Brother Fulgence seeking refuge at a distance, and shielding himself with a diplomatic illness; and Father Crabot withdrawing to his cell, where Providence had visited him with a very salutary sprain. Was it not also in order to save Gorgias that President Gragnon had illegally communicated a forgery to the first jurors, as had been proved by the evidence of architect Jacquin? Amidst the accumulation of crimes, that one alone ought to have sufficed to open the eyes of the most prejudiced. And Delbos ended by depicting the frightful sufferings experienced by Simon, the fifteen years of transportation which he had endured amidst the most cruel physical and moral tortures, while ever stubbornly raising his cry of innocence. The advocate added that, like the Procureur de la République, he also desired to have the affair ended, but ended by an act of justice which would redound to the honour of France; for if the innocent man should be struck down again, the shame of France would be indescribable, and a future full of incalculable evils would lie before her.

There was no reply from the prosecution, the case was closed, and the jury at once withdrew to its retiring-room. [4] It was about eleven o'clock in the morning, and for more than an hour the spectators remained waiting, silent and anxious, in no wise resembling the audience at Beaumont, which had been so tumultuous and violent. The hall was very hot, and the atmosphere seemed as heavy as lead. There was little conversation, though occasionally the Simonists and the anti-Simonists glanced askance at one another. One might have fancied oneself in some funeral chamber where the life or death of a nation, the whole dolorous question of its future, was being decided. At last the jury reappeared, the judges came in, and amidst lugubrious silence the foreman arose: He was a little grey, lean man, a goldsmith, enjoying the custom of the local clergy. His shrill voice was distinctly heard. On the question of guilt the verdict was 'Yes,' by a majority; while 'extenuating circumstances' were unanimously granted. At Beaumont the jury had been unanimous with respect to guilt, and only a small majority had favoured the admission of extenuating circumstances. And now, after expediting the formalities, President Guybaraud hastily pronounced a sentence of ten years' solitary confinement. That done, he withdrew, and Pacart, the Procureur de la République, followed him, after bowing to the jury as if to thank them.

> [4] At French criminal trials the judges no longer sum up the evidence before the verdict is given. That privilege was taken from them by a special law several years ago, in consequence of their scandalous abuse of it.—*Trans.*

Marc, meantime, had glanced at Simon, on whose face he only detected a kind of faint smile, a painful contraction of the lips. Delbos, beside himself, was clenching his fists. David, whose emotion was too intense, had not returned into Court, but was awaiting the decision outside. The thunderbolt had fallen, and Marc felt a deadly chill in every vein. It was a frigid horror: the supreme iniquity, in which just minds had refused to believe, the crime of crimes, which had seemed impossible a few hours earlier, which reason had rejected, had suddenly become a monstrous reality. And there were no ferocious cries of joy, there was no onslaught like that of cannibals rushing to a feast of blood, as at Beaumont. Though the hall was full of rabid anti-Simonists, the frightful silence continued, such was the horror which froze one and all to their very bones. Only a long shudder, a stifled groan, sped through the throng. And they went out without a word, without a push, in a dark stream like some funeral assembly choking with emotion, stricken with fear. And outside Marc found David sobbing.

So the Church was victorious—the Brothers' school would revive to life, while the secular school would again become the ante-room of hell, the satanic den where children were corrupted both in mind and body. The desperate and gigantic effort made by the Congregations and by almost all the clergy had again retarded their defeat, which was certain in the future. For years, however, one would again see the young generations stupefied by error, rotted by lies. The forward march of mankind would be hampered afresh until the day when free thought—invincible and still pursuing its course in spite of everything—should at last deliver the people by science, which alone could render it capable of truth and equity.

On the following evening, when Marc returned to Maillebois, exhausted by fatigue and quite heart-broken, he found a letter of three lines awaiting him: 'I have read the whole of the inquiry, I have followed the trial. The most monstrous of crimes has been committed. Simon is innocent.—*Geneviève.*'

CHAPTER IV

On the morrow, a Thursday, Marc, who had scarcely slept that night, had just risen when he received an early visit from his daughter Louise. She, having heard of his return, had escaped for a moment from her grandmother's house. And, throwing her arms wildly about her father's neck, she exclaimed: 'Oh! father, father, what a deal of sorrow you must have had, and how pleased I am to be able to kiss you!'

A big girl nowadays, Louise was fully acquainted with the Simon affair, and shared all the faith, all the passion for justice displayed by that dearly-loved father, the master whose lofty mind was her guide. Thus her cry was instinct with the revolt and despair into which she had been cast by the monstrous proceedings at Rozan.

But, on thus seeing her before him and feeling her embrace, Marc thought of Geneviève's letter, to which his sleeplessness that night had been largely due. 'And your mother,' he asked, 'do you know that she has written to me, and that she is now on our side?'

'Yes, yes, father, I know it. She spoke of it to me.... Ah! if I were to tell you of all the quarrels there were when grandmother saw mamma beginning to read everything, procuring documents which had never been in the house before, and going out every morning to buy the full report of the new trial. Grandmother wanted to burn everything, so mamma shut herself up in her own room and spent all her time there.... And I also read everything; mamma allowed me to do so. Oh! papa, what a dreadful affair—that poor man, that poor innocent, overwhelmed by so many cruel people! If I could, I should love you all the more for having loved and defended him!'

She again threw her arms about her father's neck and kissed him with heartfelt fervour. And he, in spite of his sufferings, began to smile as if some delicious balm had somewhat calmed the smarting of his wounds. And while he smiled he pictured his wife and his daughter reading together learning the truth, and at last returning to him. 'Her letter, her dear letter,' he said in an undertone, 'what consolation and hope it gave me! Will not joy return after so many misfortunes?'

Then he anxiously questioned Louise: 'So your mother spoke to you of me? Does she understand, does she regret our torments? I always felt that she would come back to me when she knew the truth.'

But the girl prettily raised a finger to her lips. She, in her turn, was smiling. 'Oh! papa,' she said, 'don't try to make me say what I can't say yet. I should be telling a falsehood if I spoke positively. Our affairs are in a good way, that is all.... Remain patient a little longer, remain confident in your daughter, who tries to be as reasonable and affectionate as you are.'

Then she gave him some bad news about Madame Berthereau. For several years the latter had been suffering from a heart complaint, which recent events seemed to have suddenly aggravated. Madame Duparque's fits of anger, the outbursts with which she made the dark, dismal little house shake at all hours of the day, proved very prejudicial to the sick woman, for they brought on shuddering and stifling fits, which she could hardly overcome. At present, in order to escape those nervous frights, she no longer went down into the little sitting-room, but remained on a couch in her bed-chamber, gazing from morn till night at the deserted Place des Capucins, with those poor, melancholy eyes of hers, in which one read such keen regret for the joys she had lost so long ago.

'Oh! we don't amuse ourselves at all now,' Louise continued. 'Mamma remains in her room, grandmamma Berthereau in hers, and grandmamma Duparque goes up and down, bangs the doors, and quarrels with Pélagie when she finds nobody to scold.... But I don't complain, for I shut myself up as well, and work. Mamma has agreed to it, you know; I shall go up for admission to the training school in six months' time, and I hope to get in.'

Just at that moment, Sébastien Milhomme, who was free that day, arrived from Beaumont, all anxiety to embrace his former master, of whose return he had heard. And almost immediately afterwards came Joseph and Sarah, who, on behalf of their mother and the Lehmanns, whom the reconviction of Simon had overwhelmed, wished to thank Marc for his heroic if vain efforts. The brother and sister related what a thunderbolt had fallen on the wretched shop in the Rue du Trou on the previous evening, when David had telegraphed the frightful tidings. Madame Simon had preferred to await them there with her parents and her children, such great hostility had she encountered in that clerical town of Rozan, where, moreover, her modest means did not allow her to live. And the mournful house was again in tears, acquainted only with the iniquitous verdict and ignorant of what might now happen, all decision as to the future being postponed until the return of David, who, for the time, had remained near his brother.

The eyes of Joseph and Sarah were still red and swollen, for they had spent a tearful, feverish night without a moment's quiet rest; and as, while speaking of their father, they again began to sob, Sébastien, carried away by his feelings, kissed his good friend Sarah, while Louise, taking hold of Joseph's hands, and likewise shedding tears, naïvely sought to console him somewhat by speaking of her great affection for him. She was seventeen and he twenty. Sébastien was a year or two older, and Sarah was eighteen. Marc felt moved as he saw those young folk there before him, quivering with youth, intelligence, and kindliness. And a thought, which had occurred to him and brought him a delightful hope already in the days when he had seen them playing as children, now returned. Might they not, indeed, be predestined consorts, such as would produce the happy harvest of the future, who would bring broader hearts and more liberal minds to the great work of to-morrow?

But although his daughter's visit gave Marc no little comfort for the time, he became very downcast on the ensuing days, so distressful was the spectacle which his poor poisoned and dishonoured country now presented. The crime of crimes had been committed, and France did not rise against it! During the long struggle for revision Marc had already failed to recognise in her the generous, magnanimous, liberating, and justice-dealing country to which he had dedicated such lofty and passionate love. But never had he thought it possible that she would sink to that base level, and become a deaf, harsh, sleepy, and cowardly France, making her bed in shame and iniquity!

How many years and generations would be needed to arouse her from that abominable somnolence? For a moment Marc despaired; he deemed his country lost; it was as if he could hear Férou's maledictions arising from the grave: 'France doomed, completely rotted by the priests, poisoned by a filthy press, sunk in such a morass of ignorance and credulity that never would one be able to extricate her.' On the morrow of the monstrous verdict of Rozan he had still imagined an awakening to be possible, he had awaited a rising of upright consciences and healthy minds; but none had stirred, the bravest seemed to hide themselves away in their corners, and the supreme ignominy took its course, thanks to the universal imbecility and cowardice.

As he went about Maillebois, Marc caught sight of Darras, who now pulled a very long face, though he was simply in despair at the mayoralty again escaping him, owing to the triumph of the clerical party. Then, on meeting Fernand Bongard, the Doloirs and the Savins, his former pupils, Marc felt greatly distressed, for he now realised, decisively, that he had been able to impart to them little if any social equity and civic courage. Fernand shrugged his shoulders, bent on knowing nothing. The Doloirs had again begun to doubt Simon's innocence; while as for the twin Savins, if they remained convinced of it, they argued that they could not effect a revolution by themselves, and that, after all, one Jew more or less was a matter of no importance. Terror reigned, people hurried home, resolved to compromise themselves no further. Things were even worse at Beaumont, whither Marc repaired to see if he could not arouse some influential people and persuade them to attempt a last effort to have the infamous verdict set aside. Lemarrois, to whom he thus ventured to apply, seemed to take him for a madman; and discarding his usual courteous kindliness, he plainly, almost roughly, told him that the affair was ended, and that any attempt to revise it would be insane, for the country was utterly sick and weary of the whole business. It had become most hurtful as a basis for political action, and if the clerical reactionaries were allowed an opportunity to exploit it any further, the Republic would certainly be undone at the approaching elections. The elections indeed! That was again the great argument. The only policy was to bury the supreme iniquity in even deeper silence than after the first trial. There was no need of any understanding to that effect. The deputies, the senators, the prefect, the officials, all sank instinctively into perfect silence, in the dread they felt at the thought of the twice condemned but innocent man. And once again former Republicans and Voltaireans like Lemarrois drew yet nearer to the Church, whose help they thought they might require to resist the rising tide of Socialism. Lemarrois, personally, had been pleased to see his adversary Delbos defeated at Rozan, and in resorting to a cowardly policy of silence he was largely influenced by a desire to let Simon's compromised champions drown themselves. Amid that general *débâcle* only Marcilly retained his amiable smile. He had already held the portfolio of Public Instruction in a Radical ministry, and felt certain of securing it again, some day, in a Moderate one. And so convinced was he now of the irresistible power of his suppleness and his freely-bestowed hand-shakes that, alone amongst those to whom Marc applied, he gave him a cordial greeting; and, without making any express promise, allowed him to hope for everything should he (Marcilly) return to power.

For the moment the Congregations became triumphant. What a relief it was to think that Father Crabot, his accomplices and his creatures, were saved! Ex-presiding Judge Gragnon gave a grand dinner, followed by a reception, to which flocked all the members of the judicial world, with many functionaries and even university men. They smiled and shook hands, well pleased at finding themselves alive after incurring such serious danger. Every morning *Le Petit Beaumontais* celebrated the victory of the valiant soldiers of God and the country. Then, all at once, it became silent, in compliance no doubt with some hint received from exalted spheres. The fact was that amid all the stir of victory everybody began to detect moral defeat. Fear of the morrow revived, and it was deemed prudent to divert people's minds.

Moreover, the Rozan jurors had now made revelations; it was known that they had convicted Simon merely by a majority of seven to five, and that on quitting the court they had unanimously signed a recommendation for pardon. They could not have confessed more plainly the mortal embarrassment in which they had been placed, the cruel necessity of confirming the former verdict of Beaumont, even though they retained little doubt of the prisoner's innocence. And the extraordinary course taken by that jury, which, in the most contradictory way, at one moment condemned Simon and at another absolved him, tended to make his innocence manifest to everybody. A pardon was felt to be so necessary and so inevitable that nobody was surprised when one was signed a few days later. *Le Petit Beaumontais* thought fit to insult the dirty Jew a last time, but even the managers of that unprincipled rag heaved a sigh of relief, glad to be at last delivered from the abominable part they had played for so many years.

David was beset by a final anguish, a frightful struggle of conscience, in connection with that pardon. His brother's strength was quite spent, fever consumed him, he was so exhausted, both physically and morally, that, doubtless, he would merely return to prison to die there. And, on the other hand, a weeping wife and children awaited him, still hoping that they might save him by dint of care and love. Nevertheless, David at first rejected the idea of a pardon, and, before everything else, wished to consult Marc, Delbos, and the other valiant defenders of the innocent prisoner; for he well understood that, even if the pardon would not deprive Simon of the right of some day establishing his innocence, it would rob the others of their most powerful means of prosecuting that cause of justice to which they had given their lives. But, however grieved they might be, all bowed to the suggestion of a pardon, and David then accepted it. At the same time it was felt by Marc and Delbos that the Congregations had good reason to be triumphant, for, humanly, the Simon affair was ended by that pardon, in consequence of which it would no longer stir the multitude to a sense of equity and generosity.

The question of Simon's future was speedily settled. It was impossible to take him back to Maillebois, where Madame Simon had decided to remain a little longer with her children, Joseph and Sarah, who were awaiting the reopening of the neighbouring training schools. David once more took everything on himself. He had long previously formed his plans, which were to dispose of his sand and gravel pits, and acquire a marble quarry in a lonely valley of the Pyrenees—an excellent affair, which a friend had recommended to him and which he had carefully studied. He meant to remove Simon thither, taking him as a partner, and assuredly the mountain air and the delight of active life would restore his health within six months' time. As soon as the installation should be effected Madame Simon might rejoin her husband, and even the children might end the vacation in their father's company. All this was carried into effect with remarkable precision and despatch. Simon was conjured away from Rozan, which was still in an agitated state, and for a time nobody even suspected that he had been removed. He travelled unrecognised, vanishing with David into that lonely valley, embosomed amid lofty peaks. It only became known by a newspaper article that his family had joined him. From that moment he altogether disappeared, and people even began to forget his existence.

On the very day when the Simon family found itself reunited in that Pyrenean solitude, Marc repaired to the Training College of Beaumont, whither an urgent letter from Salvan had summoned him. And as soon as they had shaken hands they began to talk of the Simons, evoking the sweet and touching scene which was being enacted far away—indeed at the other end of France.

'We must all take it as our reward,' said Salvan. 'If we have not yet managed to make the affair yield the great social lesson and the penalties that attach to it, we have at least brought this happiness to pass, we have restored the poor martyr to his wife and his children.'

'Yes,' said Marc, 'I have been thinking of it ever since this morning. I can picture them all together, smiling, in peace, under the broad blue sky. And, for that poor man so long fastened to his chain, what a delight it must be to be able to walk about freely, inhaling the freshness of the mountain springs, the pure odours of the plants and trees! The dear children, too, and the dear wife, how happy they must feel to see their dream realised, to have him beside them again, to take him about like a big child just recovering from a severe illness, and watch him reviving to health and strength!... You are right, it is our reward—the only one.'

He paused, then added in a lower voice with some of the bitterness of a combatant who laments that his weapon should have been broken in his hand: 'Our *rôle* is quite over. A pardon was inevitable, no doubt, but it has deprived us of all power of action. We can only wait for the crop of good grain we have sown—that is, if ever it will sprout up in the hard ground where we have scattered it.'

'Oh! it will rise, never fear, my friend,' Salvan exclaimed. 'We must never despair of our poor, great country. It may be deceived, it may deceive itself, but it always returns to truth and reason. Let us rest satisfied with our work, it will bear fruit in the future.' Then, after a pause, he continued in a thoughtful way: 'But I agree with you that our victory will not be immediate. The times are really execrable; never have we passed through a more troublous and threatening period. And, indeed, if I asked you to call to-day, it was in order to talk to you of the present disquieting situation.'

Then he acquainted Marc with what he had learnt. Since the trial at Rozan, all the recognised Simonists, all the brave men who had become compromised in the affair, had found themselves exposed to the vengeance of the Congregations, the hatred of the egotistical and cowardly multitude. Undoubtedly they would be made to pay heavily in their interests and their persons for the crime they had committed by supporting the cause of truth and justice.

'Have you heard that nobody now bows to Delbos at the Palace of Justice?' said Salvan. 'Half the cases confided to him have been withdrawn. Clients regard him as being altogether too compromising. He has to begin his career afresh; and at the next elections he will certainly be defeated again, for the affair has led to disruption even in the Socialist ranks.... For my own part, I shall probably be dismissed——'

'Dismissed? You!' interrupted Marc in accents of surprise and grief.

'Why, yes, my friend. You are not ignorant of the fact that Mauraisin has long coveted my post. He never manœuvred otherwise than in order to dislodge me. His prolonged flirtation with the Church party has been simply a matter of tactics in order to secure its support in the hour of victory. After the inquiry of the Court of Cassation he certainly felt frightened, and began to say that he had always regarded Simon as innocent. But, since Simon was reconvicted, Mauraisin has again been barking with the clerical pack, feeling convinced that Le Barazer will be compelled to dismiss me by the pressure brought to bear on him by all the victorious reactionary forces. It will astonish me very much if I am still here when the new term begins in October.'

Marc again began to express his grief; and, moreover, he refused to believe Salvan. He recalled all the services which the latter had rendered, and set forth the necessity of persevering with the great work of saving France from falsehood and credulity. 'You cannot leave before your task is accomplished,' he added; 'there remains so much for you to do. Although Le Barazer has never spoken out plainly, he has been at heart on our side, and I am sure that he will never be guilty of such a bad action as to dismiss you.'

Salvan smiled somewhat sadly. 'In the first place,' he answered, 'nobody is indispensable; I may disappear, but others will rise to continue the good work we have begun. Mauraisin may take my place, but I am convinced that he will do no great harm, for he will not retain it long, and he will be forced to follow in my footsteps. Some work, you see, when once it has been begun, is accomplished by the very force of human evolution, and remains independent of any particular, individual men.... But one might think by the way you talk that you did not know Le Barazer. We are, personally, of little account in his intricate republican diplomacy. He was on our side, that is certain; he would be with us still if we had won the battle. But our defeat has placed him into the greatest possible embarrassment. He really has but one desire, to save his work, the system of secular and compulsory education of which he was one of the creators. Thus, as the Church has regained power for the moment and threatens his work, he will resign himself to necessary sacrifices and temporise until he is able to speak as a master in his turn. Such is his nature, and we cannot alter him.'

Salvan continued in this strain, enumerating all the influences which were being brought to bear on Le Barazer. Rector Forbes, who was so desirous of quietude and who so greatly feared worries with the minister, had plainly told him that he must satisfy the demands of the opposition deputies. These, at the head of whom Count Hector de Sanglebœuf distinguished himself by his violence, were making every effort to secure the dismissal of all the notorious Simonists belonging to the civil and the educational services. And none of the Republican deputies, not even the radical Lemarrois, moved; indeed, they consented to that hecatomb in order to pacify public opinion, anxious as they were to lose as few electors as possible. At present, also, professors and masters followed the example of Principal Depinvilliers, attending Mass with their wives and daughters every Sunday. Then, at the Lycée of Beaumont, the chaplain reigned supreme; religious exercises were becoming compulsory; all pupils who refused attendance were badly noted, harassed and ill-treated until no resource was left them but to comply or quit. Father Crabot made his hand felt at that Lycée with the same reactionary authority that he displayed in the management of the College of Valmarie. And the increasing audacity of the Congregations was demonstrated by the fact that the Jesuit professors of Valmarie now openly acknowledged their standing, whereas previously, in order to defeat the laws, they had outwardly passed themselves off as secular priests.

'That is how we stand,' Salvan concluded. 'Thanks to the reconviction of Simon, they speak as masters, and wring whatever they please from the universal cowardice and imbecility.... It is already said that Mademoiselle Rouzaire is to be appointed head-mistress of the chief girls' school in Beaumont. Jauffre, now at Jonville, is also to be appointed here, it seems; for he has threatened to turn against Abbé Cognasse if there should be any further delay in rewarding his services. Finally, Doutrequin, once a

Republican, who has rallied to the Church from a deplorable aberration of patriotism, has secured two suburban schools for his sons, who have made Nationalism and Anti-Semitism their chief dogmas, so that we are now once more in a period of acute reaction—the last we shall witness, I hope, pending the day when the country will spit out the poison which is killing it.... And if I am dismissed, my friend—you suspect it, do you not?—you will be dismissed also.'

Marc smiled. He now understood why Salvan had sent for him in all haste. 'So I am condemned?' he said.

'Yes, I am afraid so; and I wished to warn you of it immediately.... Oh! the thing is not settled yet; Le Barazer remains silent, biding his time, as it were, and saying nothing of his intentions. But you can have no idea of the assaults he has to withstand, particularly with respect to yourself. Naturally enough, it is your dismissal that is most urgently demanded. I was talking to you just now of that big simpleton Sanglebœuf, that puppet whose strings are pulled by the old Marchioness de Boise, whom he drives to despair, I hear, so clumsily does he execute the movements which she directs. Well, three times already Sanglebœuf has bounced up to the Préfecture to threaten Le Barazer with an interpellation in the Chamber of Deputies if he does not come to an understanding with Prefect Hennebise to annihilate you. You would be already dead, I think, if it had not been for the arrogance of that ultimatum. But it isn't possible for Le Barazer to resist much longer, my poor friend. And you mustn't bear him any malice. Remember all the quiet obstinacy and diplomatic skill with which for many years he supported you. He always found some means of saving you by granting compensations to your adversaries. But now it is all over, I have not even spoken to him about you. All efforts on your behalf would be useless. You must let him act as he pleases. Doubtless he is only delaying his decision in order to devise something ingenious; for he himself does not like to be defeated, and he will never relinquish his efforts on behalf of his work, that system of secular and compulsory education which alone can give us a new France.'

Marc smiled no longer; indeed, he had become very sad. 'It will be a great blow,' he answered. 'I shall leave the best of myself behind me in that school of Maillebois, among those dear lads whom I regard almost as my own children.... Besides, what shall I do if my career is thus brought to an end? I am not competent to take up any other useful work, and how painful it will be to see the work I have been doing interrupted, left unfinished at the very moment when, more than ever, truth has need of sturdy workers.'

But Salvan in his turn bravely smiled, and, taking hold of Marc's hands, said to him: 'Come, don't lose your courage. We shall surely find something to do; we sha'n't remain with our arms crossed.'

Then Marc, feeling comforted, replied: 'You are right! When a man like you is struck, one can follow him into disgrace without thought of shame. The future, at all events, belongs to us.'

A few more days went by. At Maillebois the victorious Congregations were endeavouring to turn the situation to pecuniary account. Great efforts were made to restore the former prosperity of the Brothers' school, several families were won over, and it seemed likely that at the new term the school would gain a dozen fresh pupils. Meantime the Capuchins showed extraordinary audacity. Was it not, after all, the glorious St. Antony of Padua who had managed everything, obtained everything from the benevolence of heaven? Indeed, it could not be denied. It was to him that one owed the reconviction of Simon, thanks to the franc and two-franc pieces which so many pious souls had dropped into the saint's collection-boxes while asking him to bring about the annihilation of the Jew. Thus a fresh miracle had been performed. Never before had the saint's power been manifested in so lofty a manner, and as a natural result offerings poured in from all sides. Moreover, Father Théodose, encouraged, inspired by this success, conceived a masterly plan to reap another large harvest of money by the saint's aid. He launched an extraordinary financial affair with mortgage bonds on Paradise, each bond being of five francs' value. The district was flooded with circulars and prospectuses explaining the ingenious working of these investments in celestial felicity. Each bond comprised ten coupons of half a franc, representing good works, prayers, and masses payable as interest here below, and redeemable in heaven at the cashier's office of the miracle-working St. Antony. Premiums were also offered in order to attract subscribers. Twenty bonds gave one a right to a coloured statuette of the saint, and a hundred ensured one an annual Mass. Finally, the prospectus explained that the name of St. Antony's Bonds was given to this scrip, because it was the saint who would redeem it a hundredfold in the next world. And the announcement ended with these words: 'Such supernatural guarantees make these bonds absolutely safe. No financial catastrophe can threaten them. Even the destruction of the world, at the end of time, would leave them in force, or rather would at once place the holders in the enjoyment of the full capitalised interest.' [1]

> [1] As some readers might think this an invention on M. Zola's part, it is as well to mention that the prospectus referred to was actually issued by a French religious community.—*Trans.*

The success was enormous. In a few weeks' time thousands of bonds had been sold. Those devotees who were too poor to buy a whole one clubbed together, and then divided the coupons. Credulous and suffering souls eagerly risked their money in this new lottery, whose great prize was to be the realisation of a fondly dreamt-of eternity of happy life. It was certainly rumoured that Monseigneur Bergerot intended to prohibit this impudent speculation which scandalised the more reasonable Catholics; but in the unpleasant position in which the prelate had been placed by the defeat of the Simonists, whom he was accused of having stealthily supported, he was doubtless afraid to do so. Though it greatly distressed him to abandon the Church to the rising tide of superstition, he had found that he could place little reliance on his clergy, and thus he had never had the courage to resist the all-powerful Congregations. Aged as he now was, he had become weaker still, only retaining enough strength to kneel and beg God's forgiveness for thus suffering the merchants to invade the temple. But Abbé Quandieu, the priest of St. Martin's, could not bear that desecration any longer. All his Christian resignation forsook him when the so-called Bonds of St. Antony made their appearance. Such trafficking was too outrageous, and he gave expression in the pulpit to his revolt as a minister of Christ, his grief at beholding the base downfall of that great Christianity which had renewed the world, and which so many illustrious minds had raised to the purest summits of ideality. Then he paid a last visit to his Bishop and friend, Monseigneur Bergerot, and finding him unable to continue the struggle, feeling too that he himself was vanquished and paralysed, he resigned his cure and withdrew to a little house in the outskirts of Maillebois, intending to dwell there on a scanty income, outside that Church whose policy of hatred and whose basely superstitious worship he could no longer serve.

The Capuchins deemed the opportunity favourable for a fresh triumph in celebration of what Father Théodose styled the flight of their former adversary. By careful manœuvring the Bishop had been induced to appoint a young curate of the *arriviste* school, a creature of Father Crabot's, to the parish of Maillebois, and the idea was to bear a superb statue of St. Antony, all red and gold, in solemn procession from the Capuchin Chapel to St. Martin's, where it would be set up in great pomp. This would be the crowning consecration of the victory which had been achieved, the conquest of the parish by the Congregation, the monks becoming its sovereign masters, able to disseminate on every side the idolatrous worship, by which they hoped to bleed and abase the community, and turn it into the ignorant flock of the days of servitude. The procession, which took place one warm day in September, with the co-operation of all the clergy of the district, proved magnificent, and was attended by a great concourse of people who repaired to Maillebois from all points of the department. Only the Place des Capucins and a short lane really separated the chapel from the church, but a roundabout line of route was selected; they crossed the Place de la République and marched along the whole high street, in this wise promenading St. Antony from one to the other end of the town. Mayor Philis, surrounded by the clerical majority of the Municipal Council, followed the painted statue, which was borne on a platform draped with red velvet. Although it was holiday time, the whole of the Brothers' school had been mobilised, boys had been specially recruited, dressed, and provided with candles. Behind them came the Daughters of Mary and numerous pious brotherhoods, sisterhoods, and other associations, an interminable string of devotees, to say nothing of all the nuns brought expressly from the Beaumont convents. Only Monseigneur Bergerot was wanting. As it happened he had sent a letter of regret, having fallen ill two days previously.

Never before had Maillebois been possessed by such religious fever. People knelt on the foot pavements, men shed tears, three girls fell to the ground in hysterical fits, and had to be carried to a chemist's shop. In the evening the benediction at St. Martin's amid the pealing of the bells was quite dazzling. And not a doubt remained; surely the town was now redeemed and forgiven; by that grandiose ceremony Providence signified its willingness to wipe out for ever the vile memory of Simon the Jew.

It so happened that Salvan came to Maillebois that day in order to see Madame Berthereau, respecting whom he had received some extremely disquieting news. And he had just quitted the little house in the Place des Capucins when he caught sight of Marc, who, on his way home after a visit to the Lehmanns, had found his progress barred by the interminable procession. They shook hands in silence; then for some time were compelled to remain waiting. When the last of the monks had gone by behind the idol all ablaze with gilding and red paint, they just exchanged a glance and took a few steps in silence.

'I was going to call on you,' said Salvan at last.

Marc fancied that he had brought him news of his dismissal. 'Is it signed then?' he inquired. 'Am I to pack my trunks?'

'No, no, my friend; Le Barazer has given no signs of life as yet. He is preparing something.... But our dismissal is certain, you must take a little patience.' Then, ceasing to jest, he added with an expression of grief: 'The fact is, I heard that Madame Berthereau was at the last stage and I desired to see her.... I have just left her, and her end is certainly very near.'

'Louise came to warn me of it yesterday evening,' Marc replied. 'I should have liked to call at once, as you have done. But Madame Duparque has signified that she will immediately quit the house if I should dare to set foot in it on any pretext. And though Madame Berthereau, as I know, would like to see me, she is afraid to give expression to her desire, for fear of some scandal beside her death-bed.... Ah! my friend, one can never overcome the hatred of a bigot.'

They walked on, again preserving silence. At last Salvan resumed: 'Yes, Madame Duparque keeps good guard, and for a moment I thought that she would not let me go upstairs. At all events she did not quit me; she kept a watch on everything I said, either to the patient or your wife.... She is certainly afraid that something may result from the blow which is about to fall on the house. Yes, Madame Berthereau, her daughter, is about to escape from her by death, and she fears, perhaps, that Geneviève, her granddaughter, may also free herself.'

Marc halted, and, giving his friend a keen glance, inquired: 'Did you notice any sign of that?'

'Well, yes; but I did not wish to mention it to you, for it would distress me to give you any false hope.... But it was in connection with that procession, that barefaced idolatry which we witnessed just now. It appears that your wife absolutely refused to attend it. And that is why I found Madame Duparque at home. She, of course, was very desirous of displaying her piety in the front rank of all the devotees, but she feared that if she should absent herself for a single moment, you or some other soul-snatcher might get into the house and rob her of her daughter and granddaughter. So she remained at home, and you can imagine with what cold fury she received me, trying to transpierce me with those eyes of hers, which are like rapiers.'

Marc was becoming excited: 'Ah! so Geneviève refused to attend that procession! She understood its hurtfulness, its baseness and folly, then; and she is returning in some degree to the healthy common-sense she used to show?'

'No doubt,' Salvan answered. 'I believe that she felt particularly hurt by those ridiculous mortgage bonds on Paradise.... Ah! what a master-stroke, my friend! Never before was human imbecility exploited to such a degree by religious impudence.'

While conversing the friends had slowly directed their steps towards the railway station, where Salvan intended to take the train in order to return to Beaumont. He did so, and Marc, on quitting him, felt once again full of hope.

As Salvan had indeed suggested, Geneviève—in that little house of the Place des Capucins, which had become yet more mournful and frigid now that death hovered over it so threateningly—was assailed by another crisis which was gradually transforming her. At first she had been thunderstruck by the revelation of the truth, the certainty of Simon's innocence, which the perusal of all the documents had brought her—that terrible light whose blaze had revealed to her the infamy of the holy men whom she had hitherto accepted as the directors of her conscience and her heart. All came from that, doubt penetrated into her mind, faith took flight, she could not do otherwise than reflect, examine and judge everything. A feeling of disquietude had already come upon her at the time when she quitted Father Théodose; and the latter's Bonds of St. Antony, that base attempt to exploit the credulity of the public, had suddenly shown her his venality and disgusted her with him. Moreover, not only did the monk's character decline in her estimation to the lowest level, but the worship he represented—that religion which had cast her into transports of mystical desire likewise lost its semblance of holiness. What! must she accept that unworthy trafficking, that idolatrous superstition, if she desired to remain a practising Catholic, steadfast in her faith? She had long bowed to beliefs and mysteries, even when her natural good sense had covertly protested against them; but there were limits to everything. She could not countenance that flotation of shares in heaven; she refused to walk behind that St. Antony, bedaubed with red and gold and carried about like a guy or an advertisement, to increase the multitude of subscribers. And the revolt of her reason gathered additional strength when she thought of the retirement of Abbé Quandieu, the gentle and paternal confessor, to whom she had returned when the suspicious ardour of Father Théodose had alarmed her. If such a man as the Abbé felt unable to abide in the Church, such as it had been made by the clerical policy of hatred and domination, was it not certain that all upright souls would henceforth find it difficult to remain in it?

Doubtless, however, Geneviève's evolution would not have been so rapid if certain preparatory work had not been already effected in her, slowly and without her knowledge. In order that one might fully understand those first causes, it was necessary to recall the whole of her story. Inheriting much of her father's nature—tender, gay, and amorous—she had fallen in love with Marc, carried away by such ardent passion that, in order to have that modest schoolmaster as her husband, she was willing to dwell with him almost in poverty, in the depths of a lonely village. Weary, too, in her eighteenth year, of the mournful life she had led beside Madame Duparque, the idea of liberty had attracted her; and for a moment it had seemed as if she had cast aside all her pious training, for with her husband she had displayed such youthful enchantment that he had been able to think she was wholly his. Moreover, if any fears lurked within him, he had dismissed them, setting himself to worship her, imagining he would be powerful enough to recast her in his own image, and so carried away by the happiness of the hour that he deferred that moral conquest till some other time.

But her past had revived, and again he had shown weakness, delaying action under the pretext of respecting the freedom of her conscience, and allowing her to return to religious observances. All her childhood then came back, the mystical poison which had not been eliminated from her system asserted itself, and the crisis which fatally assails the souls of women nourished on errors and falsehoods arrived, her case being aggravated by her frequentation of that bigoted and domineering woman, her grandmother. Then a whole series of incidents—the Simon case, the postponement of Louise's first Communion—had precipitated the rupture between husband and wife. In Geneviève there glowed a desire for the *au-delà* of passion, a hope of finding in heaven the divine and boundless bliss promised to her formerly in her girlish days; and her love for Marc had simply become dimmed amid her dream of the ecstasies which the canticles celebrate, an ever loftier and ever deceptive delight. But in vain had others excited her, lied to her, set her against her husband, by promising to raise her to the highest truth, the most perfect felicity. The failure, the defeat she ever encountered, sprang from her abandonment of the only natural and possible human happiness; for never since that time had she been able to content her longings. She had lived, indeed, amid increasing distress without either repose or joy, however stubbornly she might declare that she had found felicity in her deceptive and empty chimeras.

Even now she did not confess in what a void she had ever remained after her long prayers on the old flagstones of chapels, her useless Communions, when she had vainly hoped to feel the flesh and blood of Jesus mingling with her own in a union of eternal rapture. But good Mother Nature each day was winning her back, restoring her a little more to health and human love; while the old poison of mysticism became in an increasing degree eliminated at each successive defeat of religious imposture. Cast for a time into great perturbation, she strove to divert her thoughts, to stupefy herself, by stern and painful religious practices in order that she might not be compelled to understand that her love for Marc had reawakened, that she craved for rest in his embrace, in the one, sole, eternal certainty which makes of husband and wife the emblems of health and happiness.

But quarrels had broken out between Madame Duparque and Geneviève, and had grown more and more frequent and bitter. The grandmother felt that her granddaughter was escaping from her. She watched her closely, made her almost a prisoner; but, whenever a dispute arose, Geneviève always had the resource of shutting herself up in her own room. There she could dwell upon her thoughts, and she did not answer even when the terrible old woman came up and hammered at the door. In this way she secluded herself on two successive Sundays, refusing to accompany her grandmother to vespers, in spite of both entreaties and threats.

Madame Duparque, now seventy-eight years old, had become a most uncompromising bigot, fashioned in that sense by a long life of absolute servitude to the Church. Reared by a rigid mother, she had found no affection in her husband, whose mind had been set on his business. For nearly five and twenty years they had kept a draper's shop in front of the Cathedral of St. Maxence at Beaumont, a shop whose custom came chiefly from the convents and the parsonages. And it was towards her thirtieth year that Madame Duparque, neglected by her husband and too upright to take a lover, had begun to devote herself more and more to religious observances. She checked her passions, she quieted them amid the ceremonies of the ritual, the smell of the incense, the fervour of the prayers, the mystical assignations she made with the fair-haired Jesus depicted in pious prints. Having never known the transports of love, she found sufficient consolation in the society of priests. And not only did she derive happiness from the unctuous gestures and caressing words of her confessor, but even his occasional rigour, his threats of hell and all its torments, sent a delightful quiver coursing through her veins. In blind belief and strict adherence to the most rigid practices, she found, too, not only satisfaction for her deadened senses, but the support and governance she needed in her weakness as a daughter of the ages. The Church knows it well; it does not conquer woman only by the sensuality of its worship, it makes her its own by brutalising and terrorising her. It treats her as a slave habituated to harsh treatment for centuries, a slave who ends by feeling a bitter delight in her very servitude.

Thus Madame Duparque, broken to obedience from her cradle days, was one of the subjugated daughters of the Church, one of those creatures whom it distrusts, strikes, and disciplines, turning them into docile instruments, which enable it to attack men and conquer them in their turn. When, after losing her husband and liquidating her business, Madame Duparque had installed herself at Maillebois, her one occupation, her one passion had become the practice of that authoritarian piety, by which she strove to remedy the spoiling of her life, and obtain compensation for all the natural joys, all the human forms of happiness, which she had never known. And the roughness with which she tried to impose her narrow, chilling faith upon her granddaughter Geneviève was due, in some degree certainly, to the regret she felt at having never experienced the felicity of love, which she would have liked to forbid her grandchild, as if it were indeed some unknown and perchance delightful hell, where she herself would never set foot.

But between the grandmother and the granddaughter there was the doleful Madame Berthereau. She likewise seemed to be only a devotee bent beneath the rule of the Church, which had taken possession of her from the moment of her birth. Never for a single day had she ceased to follow its observances. With loving weakness her husband, Berthereau the freethinker, had accompanied her to Mass. But she had also known his love, the ardent passion with which he had always encompassed her, and the recollection of it possessed her for ever. Though many years had elapsed since his death, she still belonged to him; she lived on that one memory, ending her days in solitude, in the arms of that dear shade. This explained her long spells of silence, the resigned, retiring manner she preserved in the mournful little house to which, as to a convent, she had withdrawn with her daughter Geneviève. She had never thought of marrying again; she had become a second Madame Duparque, rigidly and meticulously pious, clad invariably in black, and showing a waxen countenance, a cowed and crushed demeanour under the rough hand which weighed so heavily on the house. At the utmost a faint twinge of bitterness appeared on her tired lips, and a fugitive gleam of rebellion shone in her submissive eyes when at times the memory of her dead husband, awakening within her, filled her amid the frigid empty life of religious observances in which she agonised with bitter regret for all the old happiness of love. And of recent times only the sight of her daughter Geneviève's frightful torment, that struggle of a woman for whom priest and husband were contending, had been able to draw her from the shrinking self-surrender of a recluse taking no interest in the cares of worldly life, and lend her enough courage to face her terrible mother.

And now Madame Berthereau was near her death, well pleased, personally, by the prospect of that deliverance. Nevertheless, as her strength ebbed away, day by day, she felt more and more grieved at having to leave Geneviève struggling in torture, and at the mercy of Madame Duparque. When she herself was gone, what would become of her poor daughter in that abode of agony, where she had suffered so dreadfully already? To the poor dying woman the thought of going off like that, without doing anything, saying anything that might save her daughter, and help her to recover a little health and happiness, became intolerable. It haunted her, and one evening, when it was still possible for her to speak gently and very slowly, she mustered sufficient courage to satisfy her heart.

It was an evening in September—a mild and rainy one. Night was at hand, and the little room, which, with its few old pieces of walnut furniture, had an aspect of conventual simplicity, was gradually growing dim. As the sick woman could not lie down, for she then at once began to stifle, she remained in a sitting posture, propped up by pillows, on a couch. Although she was only fifty-six, her long sad face, crowned by snowy hair, looked very aged indeed, worn and blanched by the emptiness of her life. Geneviève sat near her in an armchair, and Louise had just come upstairs with a cup of milk, the only nourishment which the ailing woman could still take. A heavy silence was lulling the house to sleep, the last clang of the bells of the Capuchin Chapel having just died away in the lifeless atmosphere of the little deserted square.

'My daughter,' at last said Madame Berthereau in accents which came from her lips very faintly and slowly, 'as we are alone, I beg you to listen to me, for I have various things to tell you, and it is quite time I should do so.'

Geneviève, surprised, and anxious as to the effect which this supreme effort might have on her mother, wished her to remain silent. But Madame Berthereau made such a resolute gesture that the young woman merely inquired: 'Do you wish to speak to me alone, mother? Would you like Louise to go away?'

For a moment Madame Berthereau preserved silence. She had turned her face towards the girl, who, tall and charming, with a lofty brow and frank eyes, gazed at her in affectionate distress. And the old lady ended by murmuring: 'I prefer Louise to remain. She is seventeen, she also ought to know.... Come and sit here, close beside me, my darling.'

Then, the girl having seated herself on a chair by the side of the couch, Madame Berthereau took hold of her hands. 'I know how sensible and brave you are,' she said, 'and if I have sometimes blamed you, I none the less acknowledge how frank you are.... To-day, do you know, now that I am near my last hour, I believe in nothing save kindness.'

Again she paused for a moment, reflecting, and turning her eyes towards the open window, towards the paling sky, as if she were seeking her long life of dejection and resignation in the farewell gleam of the sun. Then her eyes came back to her daughter, at whom for a while she remained gazing with an expression of indescribable compassion.

'It grieves me extremely, my Geneviève, to leave you so unhappy,' she said. 'Ah! do not say no. I sometimes hear you sobbing overhead, at night, when you are unable to sleep. And I can picture your wretchedness, the battle which rends your heart.... For years now you have been suffering, and I have not had even enough bravery to succour you.'

Hot tears gathered suddenly in Geneviève's eyes. The evocation of her sufferings at that tragic hour quite upset her. 'Mother, I beg you, do not think of me,' she stammered; 'my only grief will be that of losing you.'

'No, no, my girl; each has to go in turn, satisfied or in despair, according to the life which he or she has chosen. But those who remain behind ought not to persevere obstinately in useless suffering when they may still be happy.' And joining her hands, and raising them with a gesture of ardent entreaty, Madame Berthereau added: 'Oh! my girl, I beg you, do not remain a day longer in this house. Make haste, take your children, and go back to your husband.'

Geneviève did not even have time to answer. A tall black form was before her, for Madame Duparque had slipped noiselessly into the room. Always prowling about the house, haunted by an everlasting suspicion of sin, she began to worry herself directly she was at a loss to tell where Geneviève and Louise might be. If they had hidden themselves did it not follow that they must be doing something evil? Moreover, the old woman never liked to leave them long with Madame Berthereau for fear lest something forbidden should be said. That evening, therefore, she had crept up the stairs as quietly as possible, with her ears on the alert; and, hearing certain words, she had gently opened the door, thus catching the others *in flagrante delicto*.

'What is that you say, my daughter?' she demanded, her rasping voice ringing with angry imperiousness.

The sick woman, pale already, became quite ghastly at that sudden intervention, while Geneviève and Louise remained thunderstruck, alarmed also as to what might now happen.

'What is that you say, my daughter?' Madame Duparque repeated. 'Are you not aware that God can hear you?'

Madame Berthereau had sunk back on her pillows, closing her eyes as if to collect her courage. She had so greatly hoped that she might be able to speak to Geneviève alone, and avoid a battle with her redoubtable mother. All her life long she had avoided any such collision, any such struggle, feeling that she would be beaten in it. But now she had only a few hours left her to be good and brave; and so she opened her eyes, and dared—at last—to speak out.

'May God indeed hear me, mother! I am doing my duty,' she said. 'I have told my daughter to take her children and return to her husband, for she will only find real health and happiness in the home which she quitted so imprudently.'

Madame Duparque, who waved her arms violently, had been minded to interrupt her at the first word she spoke. But awed, perhaps, by the majesty of death, which was already gathering in the room, embarrassed too by the heartfelt cry of that poor enslaved creature, whose reason and whose love were at last freeing themselves from their shackles, the terrible old lady allowed her daughter to finish her sentence. A pause, fraught with infinite anguish, then followed between those four women who were thus gathered together, and who represented four generations of their line.

There was a certain family resemblance between them; they were all tall, they had long faces and somewhat prominent noses. But Madame Duparque, now eight and seventy, and displaying a harsh jaw and rigidly wrinkled cheeks, had grown lean and sallow in the practice of narrow piety; whereas Madame Berthereau, who had reached her fifty-sixth year, showed more flesh and suppleness, in spite of her malady, and still retained on her livid face the gentleness bequeathed by the brief love which she had tasted, and which she had ever mourned. From those two solemn women, dark-haired in their younger days, had sprung Geneviève, fair and gay, refined by paternal heredity, loving and lovable, and still very charming at seven and thirty years of age. And Louise, the last, who would soon be in her eighteenth year, was in her turn a brunette, with hair of a deep gilded brown, inherited from her father, Marc, who had also bestowed on her his broad forehead, and his large bright eyes, glowing with passion for truth.

In like way one detected among those four women the progress of moral evolution. First there was the great-grandmother, a serf of the Church, one whose flesh and mind had been absolutely subjugated, who had become a passive instrument of error and domination; next there was the daughter, who had remained a practising and conquered Catholic, but who was disturbed, tortured by her brief experience of human happiness; then came the struggling granddaughter, in whose poor heart and mind Catholicism was fighting its last battle, who was almost rent atwain between the mendacious nothingness of her mystical education, and the living reality of her wifely love and motherly tenderness, who needed, too, all her strength to free herself; and finally there was the great-granddaughter, who was at last freed, who had escaped the clutch which the priest sets upon women and children, and who, all youth and health, had reverted to happy nature, to the glorious beneficence of the sunlight.

But in faint, slow accents Madame Berthereau was repeating: 'Listen, my Geneviève! Do not remain here any longer. As soon as I am gone, go away—go as speedily as you can.... My misfortunes began on the day when I lost your father. He adored me. The only hours that I ever really lived were those that I spent beside him; and I have often reproached myself for not having then appreciated them more, for in my stupidity I was ignorant of their value, and I only understood how delightful, how unique they had been, when I came here, a widow, loveless, for ever cut off from the world.... Ah! the icy cold of this house, how often has it made me shiver! Ah! the silence and the gloom in which I have gone on dying for years, not even daring to open a window to inhale a little life, so foolish and so cowardly I was!'

Erect and motionless, Madame Duparque still refrained from interrupting her daughter; but on hearing that cry of dolorous rebellion she could not restrain a gesture of protest. 'I will not prevent you from speaking, my daughter,' she said when the other paused, 'though if you have a confession to make it would be better to send for Father Théodose.... But since you were not wholly God's, why did you seek refuge in this house? You knew very well that here you would find none but God.'

'I have confessed,' the dying woman answered gently. 'I shall not go off without receiving extreme unction, for I belong to God entirely, I can only belong to Him now.... And even if I suffered so much from the loss of my husband, I never regretted having come here. Where else could I have gone? I had no other refuge. I was too closely linked to religion to attempt to seek other happiness, even for an instant. Thus I have lived the life I was bound to live.... But my daughter, in her turn, is suffering too cruelly, and I will not have her begin my sorry story over again, and fade away in the void in which I have agonised for so many years, for she is free, and she still has a husband who adores her.... You hear me, you hear me, do you not, my daughter?'

With a gesture of tender entreaty, she held out her poor waxen hands, and Geneviève fell upon her knees beside her, with big tears rolling down her cheeks, so deeply was she stirred by that extraordinary scene, that poignant awakening of love at the very hour of death.

'Mother, I beg you, mother,' she said, 'do not continue to grieve about my sufferings. You rend my heart by thinking only of me when we are all here, with the one desire to give you a little comfort, whereas you, it seems, wish to go off in despair.'

Increasing excitement had now gained possession of Madame Berthereau. Taking Geneviève's head between her hands, she gazed into her eyes and answered, 'No, no, listen to me. There is only one thing that can make me happy before I leave you, and that is a certainty that you will not lead a life of sacrifice and torture as I have done. Give me that last consolation, do not let me go without your promise.... I shall repeat what I have said as long as I have strength to do so. Leave this house of error and death, return to your home, your husband. Give him back his children, love each other with all your strength. Life lies in that, and truth, aye, and happiness also.... I beg you, my girl, promise me, swear to me that you will comply with my last desire.'

Then, as Geneviève, utterly upset, choking with sobs, gave her no answer, Madame Berthereau turned towards Louise, who, likewise distracted, was now kneeling at the other side of the couch. 'Help me, my dear granddaughter,' she said, 'I know what your views are. I have noticed your efforts to lead your mother home. You are a little fairy, a very sensible little person, and you have done a great deal to give a little quietness to all four of us.... Your mother must make me a promise, is it not so? Tell her that she will make me very joyful indeed by promising me to be happy.'

Louise had caught hold of the poor woman's hands, and kissing them she stammered: 'Oh! grandmother, grandmother, how good you are, and how I love you!... Mother will remember your last wishes, she will reflect, and act as her heart bids her, you may be sure of it.'

Madame Duparque meanwhile had not for a moment departed from her rigidity. Her eyes alone seemed to be alive in her frigid, wrinkled face. And furious anger blazed in them while she strove to restrain herself from any brutal action. At last she growled huskily: 'Be quiet, all three of you! You are unhappy infidels, rebelling against God, who will punish you with the flames of hell.... Be quiet, I tell you, don't let me hear another word! Am I no longer mistress here? You, my daughter, your illness has impaired your mind, I am willing to grant it. You, my granddaughter, have Satan in you, and I excuse you for having failed as yet to drive him out, in spite of your penitence. And you, my great-granddaughter, I still hope that when I am free to correct you I shall prevent you from going to damnation.... Be quiet, my children, I tell you. If it were not for me you would not exist! It is I who command here, and you would be guilty of yet another mortal sin if you should not obey me!'

Her stature seemed to have increased, and her voice had risen while, with fierce gestures, she thus spoke in the name of her Deity of anger and vengeance. But, in spite of her commands, her daughter, who already felt freed from her domination by the approach of death, was bold enough to continue: 'I have been obeying for more than twenty years, mother, I have preserved silence for more than twenty years; and if my last hour were not at hand, perhaps I should be so cowardly as to obey and keep silent now.... But I have gone through too much. All that has tortured me, all that I have left unsaid would choke me in my grave, and even there the cry I have stifled so long would rise from my lips.... Oh! my daughter, promise me, promise me what I ask!'

Then Madame Duparque, beside herself, exclaimed in a rougher voice: 'Geneviève, I, your grandmother, forbid you to speak!'

It was Louise who, seeing that her mother was still sobbing, waging a most frightful battle, with her face close pressed to the blanket spread over the couch, took upon herself to answer in her resolute yet deferential way: 'Grandmother, one must be kind to grandmother who is so ill. Mother also is very ailing, and it is cruel to upset her like this. Is it not right that each should act according to her conscience?'

Thereupon, without giving Madame Duparque time to intervene again, Geneviève, whose heart melted, touched as it was by her daughter's courageous gentleness, raised her head, and kissed the dying woman with intense emotion: 'Mother, mother, you may sleep in peace, I will not let you carry away any bitter thought on my account.... Yes, I promise you I will remember your desire, I promise you I will do all that my love for you may advise me to do.... Yes, yes, there is only kindness, there is only love: therein lies the only truth.'

Then, as Madame Berthereau, exhausted, but with a divine smile brightening her face, pressed her daughter to her bosom, Madame Duparque made a last threatening gesture. The twilight had now fallen, and only the pale gleam of the broad, cloudless sky, where the first stars were shining, lighted up the room; while the open window admitted the deep silence that rose from the deserted square, broken only by the laugh of a child. And as everything thus sank into a quiescence through which swept the august breath of coming death, the old woman, who in her obstinacy would neither see nor hear, added these words: 'You belong to me no more, neither daughter, nor granddaughter, nor great-granddaughter. One impelling the other, you are, all three of you, on the road to eternal damnation! Go, go! God casts you off, and I cast you off also!'

Then she departed, shutting the door roughly behind her. In the dim quiet room the mother remained agonising between her daughter and her granddaughter, all three united in the same embrace. And for a long, long while they continued weeping, their tears full of delightful comfort as well as bitter grief.

Two days later Madame Berthereau died, in a very Catholic spirit, after receiving extreme unction, as she had desired. At the church the stern demeanour of Madame Duparque, clad in the deepest mourning, was much remarked. Only Louise accompanied her. Geneviève had been obliged to take to her bed again, overcome by such a nervous shock that she seemed no longer able to see or hear. For three days longer she thus remained in bed with her face turned to the wall, unwilling to answer anybody, even her daughter. She must have suffered terribly; distressful moans escaped her, fits of weeping shook her from head to foot. When the grandmother went up to her, obstinately remaining there, lecturing her, and pointing out the necessity of appeasing the divine anger, the attacks became yet more violent, there were convulsions and shrieks. And Louise, who wished her mother to be spared any such aggravation of her torment, in the supreme struggle which was almost rending her asunder, ended by bolting the door, and remaining there as a sentinel, forbidding access to everybody.

On the fourth day came the *dénouement*. Pélagie alone managed to force an occasional entry in order to attend to certain work. Sixty years of age, with a sullen face, a large nose, and thin lips, the servant had become not only very thin, almost withered, but also insufferable in manner. Ever mumbling sour words, she actually overruled her terrible mistress, and often turned the work-girls, whom the latter engaged to help her, into the street. Madame Duparque kept her, however, for she was an old retainer, an old instrument who had always been ready at hand. Indeed, her mistress could hardly have lived if she had not had that underling, that serf beside her to extend, as it were, her domination over all around. She employed her as a spy, as the executor of base designs, and in return she herself belonged to her, having to put up with all the bad temper, all the additional worry and dolefulness with which the other filled the house.

On the morning of the fourth day, after the first breakfast, Pélagie, having gone upstairs to fetch the cups and plates, hastened down again, quite scared, and said to her mistress: 'Does madame know what is going on up there? They are packing their trunks!'

'The mother and daughter?'

'Yes, madame. Oh! they are making no secret of it. The girl goes from one room to the other, carrying armfuls of linen.... If madame cares to go up, the door is wide open.'

Frigidly, without answering, Madame Duparque went up. And she indeed found Geneviève and Louise actively engaged in packing two trunks, as if for immediate departure, while little Clément, who was scarcely six years old, sat very quietly on a chair, watching the preparations. The mother and daughter just raised their heads when the old lady entered, then went on with their work again.

A moment of silence followed; finally, Madame Duparque, not a muscle of whose face stirred, but who seemed to become yet more frigid and stern, inquired: 'Do you feel better, then, Geneviève?'

'Yes, grandmother. I have still some fever, but I shall never get well if I remain shut up here.'

'So you have decided to go elsewhere, I see. Where are you going?'

A quiver came over Geneviève, who once more raised her head, showing her eyes, which were still red with weeping: 'I am going where I promised my mother I would go. For four days past the struggle has been killing me.'

Another pause ensued. 'Your promise did not seem to me a formal one; I regarded your words as mere words of consolation,' said Madame Duparque at last. 'So you are going back to that man? You can have very little pride!'

'Pride! Ah, yes, I know, it is by pride that you have kept me here so long.... But I have had plenty of pride. Many a time, though I have wept all night long, I have refused to admit my error.... But now I understand the stupidity of my pride, the wretchedness into which I have sunk is too great.'

'You unhappy creature! Has neither prayer nor penitence been able to rid you of the poison, then? That poison is mastering you again, and it will end by casting you into eternal punishment should you relapse into your abominable sin.'

'What poison are you talking of, grandmother? My husband loves me, and, in spite of everything, I love him still. Is that poison? I have struggled for five years; I wished to give myself entirely to God; why did not God fill the aching void of my being, in which I desired to receive Him alone? Religion has satisfied me neither as to wifely happiness nor as to motherly tenderness, and if I am now going back to that happiness and tenderness, it is because of the downfall of that heaven in which I have found only deception and falsehood.'

'You are blaspheming, my girl, and you will be punished for it by the most cruel sufferings.... If the poison which has tortured you did not come from Satan, it follows that it must have come from God. Faith is forsaking you; you are on the high road to negation, to absolute perdition.'

'That is true; for months now I have believed a little less each day. I did not dare to confess it to myself, but amid all my bitterness of feeling something was slowly destroying the beliefs of my childhood and youth.... How strange it was! All my childhood full of chimeras, all my pious youth had revived within me, with all the fine mysteries and ceremonies of worship, when I first sought refuge here. But when I again endeavoured to plunge into the *au delà* of the mysteries, when I strove to give myself to Jesus amid the chants and the flowers, those dreams gradually faded, became mere deceptive fancies, in which nought of my being found contentment....

Yes, the poison must have been my training, the errors in which I grew up, which brought me so much suffering when they revived, and of which I shall only be cured when the evil ferment is completely eliminated.... Shall I ever be cured? I hardly know. There is still such strife within me!'

Madame Duparque was restraining herself, for she well understood that violence on her part would seal her rupture with the young woman and the girl, who, with the little boy, seated on his chair, listening attentively without understanding, were all that remained of her race. Thus she was minded to make a last effort, and addressing herself to Louise, she said: 'You, my poor child, are the most to be pitied, and I shudder when I think of the pit of abomination into which you are casting yourself.... If you had made your first Communion all these sorrows would have been spared us. God is punishing us for having failed to overcome your impious resistance. Yet there is still time, and what favours would you not obtain from His infinite mercy if you would only submit, and approach the Holy Table as a humble handmaiden of Jesus!'

But the girl responded gently: 'Why revert to that, grandmother? You know very well what promise I gave my father. I cannot vary in my answer; I will come to a decision when I am twenty; I shall then see if I have faith.'

'But, you unhappy, obstinate child, if you go back to that man, who has wrecked both your mother's life and your own, your decision can be told in advance! You will remain without any belief, any religion at all, like a mere beast of the fields!'

Then, as the daughter and mother deferentially preserved silence, and even resumed their packing in order to curtail a useless and painful discussion, the old lady gave expression to a last desire: 'Well, if you have both resolved to go, at least leave me the little boy—leave me Clément. He will redeem your folly, I will bring him up in the love of God, I will make a holy priest of him, and at least I shall not be alone; there will be two of us to pray that the divine anger may not fall upon you on the terrible Day of Judgment.'

But Geneviève had sprung to her feet. 'Leave Clément!' she exclaimed; 'why, it is largely on his account that I am going. I no longer know how to bring him up; I wish to restore him to his father, in order that we may come to an understanding and endeavour to make a man of him.... No, no, I am taking him with me!'

Then Louise, who also stepped forward, added very gently and respectfully: 'Why do you say that you will remain alone, grandmother? We do not wish to forsake you, we will often come to see you, every day if you will allow us. And we will love you well, and try to show you how much we desire to make you happy.'

Madame Duparque could restrain herself no longer. The flood of anger which she had found it so difficult to check flowed over and carried her away with a rush of furious words: 'That's enough! Keep quiet! I will listen to you no longer! But you are quite right, pack your boxes and be off! Be off, all three of you, I cast you out! Go and join that cursed man, that bandit who spat on God and His ministers to endeavour to save that filthy Jew, who has been twice condemned!'

'Simon is innocent!' cried Geneviève, in her turn losing all restraint; 'and those who caused him to be condemned are liars and forgers!'

'Yes, yes, I know; it is that affair which has ruined you and is separating us. You imagine the Jew to be innocent; you can no longer believe in God. But your imbecile justice is the negation of divine authority. And for that reason all is quite over between us.... Go, go as quickly as possible with your children! Don't soil this house any longer, don't bring any more thunderbolts upon it! You are the sole cause of its misfortunes.... And, mind, don't set foot here again; I cast you off, I cast you off for ever! When once you have crossed the threshold you need never knock at the door, it will not be opened to you. I have no children left, I am alone in the world, and I will live and die alone!'

As she spoke, the old woman, nearly in her eightieth year, drew up her lofty figure with a fierce energy. Her voice was still strong, her gestures were commanding ones. She cursed, she punished, she exterminated after the fashion of her Deity of wrath and death. And afterwards she descended the stairs with a pitiless tread, and shut herself in her room, waiting there till the last children of her flesh should be gone for ever.

It so happened that Marc, that very same day, received a visit from Salvan, who found him in the large classroom, which was quite bright with the glow of the September sunshine. The vacation would come to an end in another ten days, and, though Marc hourly expected to be informed of his dismissal, he was consulting his books and notes as if preparing for the new school year. However, by Salvan's grave if smiling demeanour, he at once understood the truth.

'This time it's done, is it not?' he exclaimed.

'*Mon Dieu*, yes, it's done, my friend. Quite a long list of changes, appointments, and promotions, prepared by Le Barazer, has been signed.... Jauffre will leave Jonville and come to Beaumont, which is fine advancement for him. That clerical Chagnat goes from Le Moreux to Dherbecourt, which is scandalous when one remembers what a brute the fellow is.... For my part, I am simply pensioned off to make room for Mauraisin, who triumphs.... And you, my friend——'

'I am dismissed, eh?'

'No, no, you have simply fallen into disgrace. You are sent back to Jonville in the place of Jauffre, and Mignot, your assistant, who is compromised with you, is to take Chagnat's post at Le Moreux.'

Marc raised a cry of happy surprise: 'But I am delighted!'

Salvan, who had come expressly to acquaint him with the news, indulged in a hearty laugh. 'That is Le Barazer's diplomacy, you see! That is what he was preparing, when, according to his habit, he endeavoured to gain time. He has ended by satisfying that terrible Sanglebœuf and all the other reactionaries by appointing Mauraisin to succeed me, and promoting Jauffre and Chagnat. And this has enabled him to retain your services and those of Mignot. Outwardly he seems to blame you, but he does not intend to disown you entirely. Besides, he is leaving Mademoiselle Mazeline here, and in your place is appointing Joulic, one of my best pupils, a man of free and healthy mind. Thus Maillebois, Jonville, and Le Moreux will be henceforth provided with excellent masters, ardent missionaries of the future.... That is the position, and, I tell you once again, nobody can alter Le Barazer; one must take him as he is and feel pleased, even when what he does is only half of what one would like to see.'

'I am delighted,' Marc repeated. 'It was more particularly the prospect of having to quit the profession altogether that grieved me. Thinking of the new term I felt sorrowful all this morning. Where could I have gone, what could I have done? It will certainly pain me to leave the boys here, for I am very fond of them. But my consolation will be to find others yonder, to whom I shall also become attached. And as for the humbleness of the school, what does that matter if I am able to continue my life-work and still sow the seed which alone can yield the harvest of truth and equity? Ah! yes, I shall go back to Jonville right willingly, and with fresh hope.'

Then he strode gaily about the bright, sunshiny classroom as if again taking on himself that teaching mission, the relinquishment of which would have been so hard to bear. And at last, with juvenile ardour and delight, he flung his arms about Salvan and embraced him. At that same moment Mignot, who, also expecting dismissal, had been seeking a situation for some days past, came in, worried at having encountered another refusal on the part of the manager of a neighbouring factory. But when he learnt that he was appointed to Le Moreux, he likewise gave expression to his joy. 'Le Moreux! Le Moreux! a real land of savages!' said he. 'No matter, one will try to civilise them a little. And we sha'n't be separated, the distance is less than three miles. That, you know, is what pleases me most of all!'

But Marc had now calmed down, and, indeed, sorrow was reviving in him, dimming his eyes once more. Silence fell, and the others could feel a quiver pass—the quiver of hope deferred, of a heart-pang which was ever keen. How hard would be the battle that Marc still had before him, how many more tears must he shed before he regained his lost happiness! At that thought he, and the others also, preserved silence; and Salvan, unable to give his friends any further comfort, sank into a sorrowful reverie as he stood gazing through the large sunlit window which faced the square outside.

But all at once he exclaimed: 'Why, are you expecting somebody?'

'Expecting somebody?' rejoined Marc, at a loss to understand.

'Yes, here comes a little hand-cart with some trunks on it.'

At that same moment the door opened, and they turned round. It was Geneviève who came in, holding little Clément by the hand, and having Louise also beside her. The surprise and the emotion were so great that at first nobody spoke. Marc was trembling. But Geneviève, in a halting voice, began at last: 'My dear Marc, I have brought you back your son. Yes, I give him back to you—he belongs to you—he belongs to us both. Let us try to make a man of him.'

The boy had stretched out his little arms, and the father caught him up wildly, and pressed him to his heart, while the mother, the wife, continued: 'And I have come back to you with him, my good Marc. You told me that I should bring him back, and come back myself.... It was truth that first conquered me; then all that you had set in me germinated, no doubt, and I have no pride left.... And here I am, for I still love you.... I vainly sought other happiness, but only your love exists. Apart from us and our children there is only unreason and wretchedness.... Take me back, my good Marc! I give myself to you as you give yourself to me.'

Thus speaking, she had slowly drawn near to her husband, and she was about to cast her arms around his neck when Louise's gay voice was heard: 'And I, and I, father! I must share in it too, you know. You must not forget me.'

'Yes, indeed, she must share in it, the dear girl!' said Geneviève. 'She strove so much to bring about this happiness, she showed such gentleness and skill.'

Then she caught Louise also in her embrace, and kissed both her and Marc, who was already holding Clément to his heart. All four were at last reunited, held in the same bond of flesh and love, having but one heart, one breath between them. And what a quiver of deep humanity, of fruitful and healthy joy now filled that large classroom, which looked so bare and empty, pending the return of the boys for the new term! Big tears welled into the eyes of Salvan and Mignot, whom emotion quite upset.

At last Marc was able to speak, and his whole heart rose to his lips: 'Ah! my dear wife, as you return to me you must at last be cured. I knew it would be so. You turned to more and more rigid religious practices as to stronger and stronger stupefacients for the purpose of sending your nature to sleep; but, in spite of everything, nature was bound to eliminate the poison when at last you again felt that you were a wife and a mother.... Yes, yes, you are right: love has delivered you; you are won from that religion of error and death, from which human society has suffered for eighteen centuries past.'

But Geneviève quivered again, becoming anxious and disturbed. 'Ah! no, no, my good Marc, do not say that! Who can tell if I am really cured? Never, perhaps, shall I be cured completely.... Our Louise will be entirely free, but the mark set on me is ineffaceable, I shall always be afraid of relapsing into those mystical dreams.... And if I have come back, it is to seek a refuge in your embrace, and to enable you to complete the work that has begun. Keep me, perfect me, try to prevent anything from ever separating us again!'

They caught each other in a tighter clasp: it was as if they were but one. Even as Geneviève had said, was not that the great work which needed to be accomplished—the work of taking woman from the Church, and setting her in her true place as companion and mother, by the side of man? For only the freed woman can free man: her slavery is ours.

But all at once Louise, who a moment previously had disappeared, opened the door again, bringing with her Mademoiselle Mazeline, who entered breathless and smiling. 'Mamma,' said the girl, 'mademoiselle must have a share in our happiness. If you only knew how she has loved me, and how kind and useful she was here!'

Geneviève stepped forward and embraced the schoolmistress affectionately. 'I knew it,' she said. 'Thank you, my friend, for all you did for us during our long worries.'

The good woman laughed, with tears in her eyes. 'Oh! don't thank me, my dear. It is I who am grateful to you for all the happiness you give me to-day.'

Salvan and Mignot were also laughing now. More handshakes were exchanged. And as Salvan, amid the babel of voices which burst forth, informed the schoolmistress of the appointments signed the previous day, Geneviève raised a cry of joy.

'What! we are going back to Jonville? Is it really true?... Ah! Jonville, that charming, lonely village where we loved each other so well, where we first lived together so happily! What a good omen it is that we are going back there, to begin our life afresh in affection and quietude! Maillebois made me feel nervous, but Jonville is hope and certainty.'

Renewed courage and infinite confidence in the future were now upbuoying Marc, filling him with superb enthusiasm. 'Love has returned to us,' said he; 'henceforth we are all-powerful. And even though falsehood, iniquity, and crime triumphed to-day, eternal victory will to-morrow be ours.'